# THE APOSTATE; OR, ATLANTIS DESTROYED. A TRAGEDY IN FIVE ACTS

*and*

# THE NEW ATLANTIS; AN AMERICAN LEGEND

By John Galt

*and*

# THE CAPTIVE

By Susanna Strickland (Moodie)

Edited and Introduction by David J. Knight
Foreword by Dr. T. Berto
Afterword by Nick Ford

Vocamus Editions
Guelph, Ontario

John Galt's *The Apostate; Or, Atlantis Destroyed* was first published in 1814, in the *New British Theatre* (Number 12, Volume 3; Pp. 305-345). The anonymous "Remarks on The Apostate" appeared following the 1814 play (Pp. 346-348). John Galt's *The New Atlantis; An American Legend* appeared in the 1831 *Friendship's Offering: A Literary Album, and Christmas and New Year's Present* (Smith, Elder; Pp. 217-229). Susanna (Moodie) Strickland's *The Captive* also appeared in the same volume of *Friendship's Offering* (Pp. 184-186).

Editing and Introduction by David J. Knight

Foreword by T. Berto

Afterword by Nick Ford

Cover image by Sona Mincoff

Cover design by Liz Morant

978-1-928171-52-2 (pbk)
978-1-928171-49-2 (ebk)

Vocamus Editions
130 Dublin Street, North
Guelph, Ontario, Canada
N1H 4N4

www.vocamus.net

2017

In Memory of

The Chonnonton First Nation

Who lived until the early 1650s where Guelph is now situated.

They were given the moniker *Attawandaron* ("Those whose speech is awry") by the Wyandot (Wendat).

This new edition is launched in April 2017, celebrating the 190th Anniversary of John Galt's foundation of Guelph.

# ACKNOWLEDGEMENTS

I would like to thank my parents and the generosity of those who have made this book possible, especially Jeremy Luke Hill of Vocamus Press (Guelph), and Jennifer Lowe (Stirling, Scotland) for her ongoing enthusiastic encouragement. I would also like to thank Liz Morant for the cover design, Sona Mincoff for the cover oil painting *Spirit Walk* (2006), Dr. T. Berto (University of Guelph) for writing the Foreword, Nick Ford (Southampton, U.K.) for writing the Afterword, and Leanne Piper (Guelph) for her historical knowledge of early Guelph quarries.

# TABLE OF CONTENTS

# FOREWORD

Dr. T. Berto
Post-colonial Inklings in John Galt's
*The Apostate; Or, Atlantis Destroyed.*

As an avid student of both history and theatre, and also a Guelph local familiar with the varied resume of John Galt, the man's 1814 play
*The Apostate; Or, Atlantis Destroyed* comes as somewhat of a surprise.
While the play appears informed by several trends contemporary to
its era of playmaking – which in themselves are interesting studies –
it also, more strikingly, operates as a subtle critique of colonial enterprise. In light of Galt's legacy as an agent of Great Britain's project
of colonial invasion, this aspect of the play is somewhat unexpected.
Galt is known for his numerous entries into the public record and
history ledgers as the subject of political, commercial, and artistic
ventures. Looking solely to his broad range of enterprises, interests,
and dabblings, one might imagine him remembered as a polymath
of great renown, that is if it weren't for the various failures that
pepper his career. Foremost Galt is best known as the founder of
Guelph, Ontario. Rather than being a landed investor, or a home-
steader converting natural landscapes into European-styled farms,
his role in the creation of Guelph was as a bureaucrat. An agent of
the Canada Company, his interpretation of his mission with Guelph
was not to survey, parcel, and sell off land to European enterprisers
with the expected evolution of a colonial village slowly expanding to
a town and so forth. Instead Galt wanted an instant city, and brought
forth numerous unorthodox schemes and ideas in his creating of the
Royal City. And while Galt's tenure in Guelph was relatively brief,
his record of city-building can be considered as inspired, questionable, or at worst, larcenous. We will never know how his various
fiscal gimmicks may have turned out in the long term – as something akin to Ponzi schemes or as brilliantly creative financing – as

he was recalled after only a short time there. What is so interesting about the man is the vigour with which he tried to bring Guelph into realisation. Indeed, in the name of his enterprises he risked his reputation, his place in the new world, and ultimately his freedom (he was jailed briefly after his return to Britain for debts). Herein lies the intrigue found in his *Atlantis*. It is fascinating that a man who so wholeheartedly appeared to be captaining colonial enterprise should write a play that questions some of the fundamental tenets beneath that project.

Atlantis has been a muse upon which writers have proposed their ideas about Euro-centricity since Plato first brought it to the public's consciousness. Plato's allegory of a mythic society, situated west of the 'known' historic world, has been fodder for a number of creations throughout history, including during the renaissance. Francis Bacon wrote his *New Atlantis* almost 200 years prior to Galt, at a time when colonial enterprise was just getting off the ground. And, while European ships had been dispatched to all habitable continents for the purposes of invasion or commerce at the time of its writing, Bacon's work is profoundly informed by the unknown-ness of what lay over the horizon. In the two centuries in between, the world had become much more known to the European invader. Colonialism had become, rather than a risky experiment, a foundational instrument in expanding the notion of the nation state further into the larger realm of empire. Various systems and ideologies had been brought into place to justify the numerous invasions, enslavements, and plundering that supported and paid for colonial enterprise. It is strange then, to find how Bacon's and Galt's versions of the myth reflect their respective times. The former's work proposes a utopia based on a place wherein a Christian Bible magically arrives. This 'miracle' should come as no surprise, as Christian indoctrination is oft considered part-and-parcel of the colonisation project. The symbiotic relationship between "the Bible and the flag" was exemplified by missionaries whom Silverman casts as the "ideological shock troops for colonial invasion" (Stanley 12) (Silverman 144). In contrast, Galt's utopia is shown as fully formed before the contagion from the East arrives, and now appears in peril because of it. It is the introduction of Christianity – in the form of the shipwrecked Antonio – that begins to destroy the island Eden and its nature-based theological system. Conversely, in Bacon's world appears a highly organised and inductive apparatus for the understanding and furthering the conquest of nature. The European developments in Galt's paradise, which arrived with Antonio, are seen instead as harbingers of an imported peril, one that steadily eats away at an ancient way of life. Galt's condemnation of the invader's culture subsuming the original is at times blunt and at others delicately understated. He shapes his critiques through variety of perspectives and presents them using a number of devices. Among these he offers various metaphors, and a set of binaries, or contrasts which, while they offer that both poles of a nature-versus-industry spectrum are perhaps extreme (and accordingly require further consideration), nevertheless suggest that the pre-colonial condition ought be revered.

As the play begins, its island world appears to teeter between a paradise – the natural splendour of the old ways – and the new, colonial production growing in its midst. European edifices of prisons and churches are being built, the physical form of the land is changing, and the enterprise of this transformation brings with it "the social arts – The various pleasures industry makes ours" (Galt II, 1: 273-274). A "tow'ring city," with "ensigns of arts and polity" form a "new magnificence" in the land (Ibid.: 258-259). All these developments appear wrought from Antonio's attempts to Christianise Atlantis. Following his shipwreck and introduction to the island, we learn that he and his vast knowledge of European culture was embraced by King Yamos (who subsequently then converted to Christianity). The king has since endeavoured to bring the rest of his people along with him, constructing as much of Antonio's prescription for a Christian society as can be done. However, the revolution is neither complete nor satisfying; Yamos still needs to rely on the old priest of the "ancient religion," Orooko, to mend his troubled relationship with his queen, Idda (I, 1). As much as Yamos revels in the newly built wonders of Antonio, he is equally troubled by a new discomfort as his wife has grows progressively more estranged. And while various causes are suspected by the king as the root of her disaffection, we see that her wonderment of Antonio's unfamiliar manners is what has changed her heart (I, 3).

The king's soldier, Arak is also experiencing a troubled love-life. His love Mora, like Idda, has also turned her affections away from her man. Both men suffer from the same unexpected allure that Antonio, and his foreign ways, have over these women. And, while it is upon Antonio's enchanting of women that the plot pivots, it is through the various ways that Galt frames Antonio, and his place in Atlantis that I find most interesting. Signs of trouble brewing in the kingdom illustrate the problems of the island's transition to Antonio's making, and thus to the status, at least in design, of a European colony. Galt's rhetoric here builds a dialectic in a series of opposing constructs in order to define his clashing worlds. And, it is in these that, at least through a contemporary lens, the validity and purpose of colonialism is examined and questioned.

From its first scene, the play sets up a broad conflict. The first line reveals a reverence for the wonders of nature, where the "calm magnificence of mountain, lake, and wood... sooth" and "charm" those in its midst (I, 1, 1-5). Nature's champion Orooko, is found revelling there in its splendour. Here, and over the course of the play, the author variously describes Orooko's understandings of his world in order to reveal the original, native creed of the land. His spirituality seems to be of Galt's invention, but with obvious resonances with various indigenous peoples within Euro-colonialism's reach. When Orooko is met by a former acolyte Arak, now a converted Christian, the priest tries to reject his former friend, but cannot. Instead he is moved by his feelings, and claims that if his friend approaches in penitence, that he may "come to my heart" (I, 1, 31). Tolerance and forgiveness are thus underscored in his relations with new apostates. While this may be construed as a singular measure of a harmonious society, more is revealed. His creed is further described as one that has never had "civil discord," but rather created "happy tribes" in its midst (I, 1, 39-40). He reminisces that until recently, theft was unknown among his faith, "nor any danger in the form of man" (I, 1, 54). However, the arrival of "the sea outcast" (Antonio) has now changed that world (I, 1, 58).

The Euro-Christian ways introduced by Antonio are framed in opposition to those of Orooko's aboriginal faith. Antonio's presences are first described by Arak for their technological advances. Antonio taught them to be bettered "tenfold," (I, 1, 59) and "to rear the safe and shelt'ring shed" (I, 1, 60) (indicating a newer, more robust form of construction). However no indication is shown that citizens were previously imperiled without such architecture. That is, other than by the threat of "the dread Gods... secret throne of fires (from) deep in the hollow of the Mountain" – presumably volcanic activity – by which Antonio's structures would still be swept away (I, 1, 70-71). Nevertheless King Yamos embraces the "new designs" (I, 1, 66) seen in "rising towns" (*The New Atlantis*, page 77) about the kingdom, all of which stem from Antonio's "Creative genius" (I, 2, 136). A typical European colonial undertaking is thus clearly reflected in Antonio's ventures.

In regards to these, the King is dismayed that his enthusiasm is not shared by all in his kingdom. To Orooko, the presence of Antonio's designs "slight the ancient rites" (I, 1, 86) of Atlantis, and Orooko fears a retribution from nature in the form of the aforementioned "fires... (which) will burst the earth, and sweep in floods of flame, Th' apostates and their perishable homes" (I, 1, 70-73). Of note here is how Galt's characterisation of Euro-colonial influence, and the native reaction to it, uses the invader's architecture and infrastructure to signify his ideological presence. While Christianity creeps across Atlantis, it appears visibly manifested in the form of European architecture.

Antonio constructs other changes in the ancient kingdom. He introduces "the all-cementing harmony of law," (I, 2, 106) complete with the concept of penal retribution. The "all-cementing" descriptor suggests that to some degree citizens' civil liberties are to be controlled as persons become subject to a power not of Gods, but of man-created laws. The introduction of such laws is manifest again through architecture. It is seen notably in the form of a prison; one that is "Too closely strong, even for the fiercest beasts," as Orooko describes it (II, 1, 286). He warns sharply against it, telling Yamos that his

"new-found arts...
...have taught you to prepare
Abodes for men, men worse than savage beasts;

If in a few short moons all these are needful,
Think what shall rise when future ages come."
(Galt II, 1, 329-334)

His admonishments clearly suggest that it is the changes to Atlantis itself, the rapid rejection of the original ways of life that will
turn citizens towards such criminality. The apparent excesses in the
prison's scale and erection are suggestive of a projection of power
intended to dwarf human significance. Its oppressive enormity is
only matched by the construction is the "too great, too lofty" (I, 2,
284) temple for the King's new "religious rites" (I, 2, 289). Orooko
laments that its massive edifice is useless to any man and instead
ponders whether it is designed to contain the Christian god himself,
where he may "Live like a creature local and limited" (I, 2, 291). When
King Yamos counters that his new god is the "God of Nature, The
spirit of the ocean and the earth!," (I, 2, 292-293) Orooko asks then
why he needs a house. Their diatribe is of interest as when Yamos
attempts to assert the Christian deity as one that is all encompass-
ing of nature, Orooko counters by re-inscribing his own god as one
where

"the whole universe is full of him
In light and blossoms, and melodious sounds,
We know his beauty; in the fruits and sleep,
And in the gladness of the blameless breast,
We feel his bounty and enjoy his care;
The skies so vast and inaccessible,
With their infinitude of stars attest
To us his greatness; in the strength of hills,
The deep foundations of the steadfast earth
And the long fetching of his breath in tempests,
We own his mighty power; and when we question
Why we do live and all this world should be,
We recognise his undiscover'd Nature."
(Galt I, 2, 294-307)

The contrast between Orooko's casting of an all-reaching and integrated natural spirit with Yamos's opulent, constructed "house" is wide. One wonders, were it not for the suggestion that they may actually be the same god, if to a reader in 1814 the discourse might verge on blasphemous.

Other sets of opposing values are illustrated throughout. Antonio's way offers "gay trappings of civilisation" manifest as "gaudy garments" while the old creed's "virtues need no robes, they ever move In healthy vigor, naked like your sires" (I, 2, 277-280). The "savage nature" of passion and "base desires" is opposed by Antonio's "purer thoughts" or so it seems (II, 2, 359-360). It is in this realm of desire and lust that Galt's most realised metaphor operates. As the women of the island begin to fall for the alien and his influences, their condition becomes expressed as a "disease" (II, 3, 390). This is asserted as an "ill," a "malady," and perhaps most interestingly as an "infection" (II, 3, 394-398). Likewise a "cure" and "remedy" are sought (II, 3, 408 and 420). While Orooko tries "With herbs and simples to relieve your ail," the affliction is far too strong for him to cure (II, 3, 457). Even though germ theory would not have been accepted widely by the public at the point of the play's creation, Galt's metaphor of the colonist and his affect as a disease is inspired. The permanence in its alteration of native cultures, the decimation of ways of life, and the failure to contain its spread all have deep resonances with Europe's sprawling colonial ventures around the globe at the time.

The disease is initially rationalised as only being ecstatic devotion. After all, Antonio's ways are so profound, so holy, that of course his new disciples fall enraptured. After all Christianity and the bible normalise rapturous ecstasy as an occasional consequence of an intimate relationship with God. However, the king doesn't initially realise the nature or source of the particular affliction, and after Orooko fails, even asks Antonio himself if he can return his wife's affections to him. Meanwhile the women's passion for Antonio soon becomes unseemly, and appears corrupted. Idda claims "some foul vapor hath beset my brain, And stain'd the wonted substance of my thoughts" (I, 3, 185-186). So bewitched has she become she claims,

"But my fit comes – ...
...o'er my head
Methinks some hideous and unholy thing
Hath perch'd itself, and feeds upon my brain."
(Galt I, 3, 240-242)

Mora, the object of Arak's affection, has likewise been afflicted. "(F)air Mora droops, And all our wonted medicines have fail'd" (I, 3, 213-214). She is left "without hope of cure" (II, 2, 377). As the play progresses, the king continues to seek the cause of his wife's misplaced passions.

For his part, Antonio considers the kingdom in an "infant state" and avoids involvements with women, lest their "soft endearments" sink his "ennobling aims" (I, 2, 146 and 148). He disdains the king's offering of the young woman Mora, presumably for his bed, as he desires a much greater price for his influence. His disaffection for her and later, other women of the kingdom is perhaps a reference to the celibacy of Catholic missionaries. Galt however has added a sinister touch to this rejection. He claims he eschews these women as they would interfere with his plans to seek a historical, if not mythical legacy. So invested is he in his colonial enterprise that he justifies all cultural disruptions by claiming that, when other colonial venturers later "come and find the arts of Europe in sweet communion with the Christian faith" in the kingdom, will he then have his name equal to Cadmus and Bacchus; equal in that they too brought "truth" westward (I, 2, 127-131). When probed further about both the fact that "The rights of father, husbands, sons, and men (he) hast prescribed to us" and about the suggestion that he live in a connubial state to give his teachings example, the apparent hypocrisy of his position becomes clear. He claims he refuses to take a mate lest he not live up to the teachings on sexual and marital matters that he has enforced on his converts. This irony is familiar to any of us that were raised Catholic – where celibate men attempt to be authoritative on matters of sexuality with which they are expected to have no such experience. However, in the era and contexts of the play's original publication, the meaning is broad. How dare the agent of colonial enterprise dictate ways of being, when they fail to live up to their own such principles? One is reminded of how the colonial project, with its supposed Christian underpinnings and divine rationalisations, so often failed to acknowledge or even atone for the sins of slavery, prostitution, and genocide that were consistent ingredients of its operation. Galt's critique here only sets the stage for further censure.

As a self-appointed missionary, Antonio's desire for legacy appears as perhaps the basest of justifications for his evangelism. In a way, his revealing of his motivations takes off a mask where without such an action, a nineteenth century audience might have held him in its esteem. As a kind of *hamartia*, or tragic flaw, we see the hubris of the selfish rationalisation for his proselytising. However, to our contemporary eyes, he can easily be read as more a metonym for the entire colonial undertaking – including its Christian buttressing. In this perspective he might be said to be standing in for God himself. Expanding on this point of view, his works would then be intended to be considered as reflexively promoting the greater glory of God, a common enough trope throughout Christendom, and one that seemingly needs no other rationale. When examined in this regard, this justification for colonial invasion appears as no more than a tautology, a ruse to promote Christian hegemony, for no other reason than its own sake.

Antonio proves to have one more mask to remove. Early in the play he tells the audience in an aside,

> "How the pure fancies of this guileless race
> Make the foul odium of my guilt appear!
> They look on me as on the orb of day;
> O little think they that the light they worship
> Gleams but from dead and guilty rottenness,
> Compar'd to which they are themselves Heaven's stars."
> (Galt II, 4, 487-492)

At this point we, as audience, are left to wonder what guilt Antonio suffers under. The plot lurches forward and Orooko offers a reason for Antonio's guilt. Without evidence, the priest makes claims that the queen has been "false" with Antonio (III, 2, 630).

However, Yamos refuses to believe it and has doggedly determined that even

> "If this Antonio be the wretch you think;
> If Idda be the victim of his guile; (*sic*)
> What may ensue? – Nothing more ill than is!
> And the good springing from Antonio's knowledge
> Must still be good, let him be what he may."
> (Galt III, 2, 683-687)

Yamos remains unconvinced and sends Orooko on his way. We still have real understanding of the source of Antonio's guilt. However a clue is revealed when he finds Idda alone in a chamber. He comments,

> "But for the woman's sympathetic lewdness
> Stirring the vice in me that I had quell'd,
> I might have left, in this new world, a name
> To match the brightest of antiquity."
> (Galt III, 3, 736-739)

Thus we learn that his claims of disinterest in sex are false, and his much prized legacy, as a result, is now in jeopardy. Later in the same scene he offers more vague explanations –

> "I dread myself – O rather let me say
> I have done that which I cannot undo,
> And by the guilt made awful forfeiture
> Of the high destiny that once was mine.
> This having done, and from all honor driven,
> I know not what extremity of guilt
> My out-cast doom may draw me yet to do."
> (Galt III, 3, 756-762)

– Yet we are still no further informed of his crime. Finally at the top of Act IV, when Antonio reflects on the situation, all is revealed.

"The sin was Nature's when she made me thus: –
These limbs she moulded; link'd the vital chain
Of lively pulses circling through my heart;
Gave that love-darting lustre to my eyes
Which the fond fair so willingly obey;
And tun'd my voice to that persuasive mood,
Which wins so easily whate'er I ask: –
Can I then doubt the promptings of desire,
Come not as issue and effect from Nature,
And if they do so, wherein lies the ill?
I cannot choose, when beauty meets my sight,
But instantly to feel its thrilling charm
Enticing to embrace. Good is but pleasure,
And that which pleases must be good to me;
If others find it harm, is the fault mine?"
(Galt IV, 1, 863-877)

His sin is thus revealed as a natural, and seemingly uncontainable ability to allure. It is in his eyes, his limbs, his voice, as "an error of my blood"; his very being causes lust amongst those around him. His 'crime' here is of interest for two reasons (IV, 1, 885). The first is how it returns to the themes of nature and natural processes – ideas about which his Christian instruction had previously advocated are controllable and can be replaced by "purer thoughts" (II, 2, 359). His failure to control them as such, and now his apparent embrace of 'natural' impulses can be read as a failure of the doctrines that lay behind them, and of course, by extension, the colonial project in itself. That is to say if Antonio, in evidence as an efficient and accomplished exemplar of a Christian movement to convert the world's peoples, cannot live up to his own ideologically determined proscriptions, how then can any empirical enterprises founded upon such ideologies hope to succeed? Secondly, his crime suggests a metaphor of the influence a foreign technology may have over another's culture. His allure is unable to be resisted among the women he instructs. His monologue above shows his allure as located in the physical beauty of his body, in his voice, and in his *gestus*. History tells us how remarkable or beautiful objects, when introduced to a culture unfamiliar with them, may gain disproportionate value due to the newness of their aesthetic uniqueness, or their previously unknown utility. Colonialism has used this as a basis for exchanges throughout centuries. We see this often in places where, for example, metal tools are introduced to cultures without metallurgy, or when advances in dye or textile technology make trinkets a form of currency, the exchange often strongly in the favour of the introducers of those objects. While complicating the idea of a new, desired 'object' with Antonio's sexual allure is problematic, we might consider the exchange that Antonio offers – one where the women acquire an unrelenting want for the object, and he gains access to power and control over their society's development – as absurdly unbalanced. Thus the play can be said to warn of one of the consequences that new presences have among colonised, often naive peoples. While this metaphor is perhaps stretched, one could certainly expand on it, if it is considered that Galt could have imagined Atlantis's citizens as non-European, that is, not white. Ideas of power dynamics, exoticism, and the sexual consequences of race in colonialism have been examined to great detail by various scholars, notably Franz Fanon in his *Black Skin, White Masks* (1952) and *The Wretched of the Earth* (1961). Exploring *Atlantis* through this frame likely would lead to further discoveries.

There are numerous other sites in *The Apostate; Or, Atlantis Destroyed* that are rich for investigation. The play's conclusion, unsurprisingly replays an all too familiar misogyny where Idda is executed and Antonio is not (he takes his own life). The five act structure plays interestingly into both Horace's and Freytag's models (as illuminated in *Die Technik des Dramas*, 1872). The narrative path that leads from Idda's enchantment to her death, without any real evidence, has resonances with both Elizabethan plots and the era's nascent form of melodrama. There are also a number of Shakespearean and biblical references to be examined. For a 21$^{st}$ century audience, where the presumed hegemony of both the church and the state are less apparent in many citizens' lives than they were in 1814, there is great opportunity to examine Galt's work unfettered by the ideological constraints under which it must have been written. As the history of colonialism is still being written, and rewritten, an examination of

# FOREWORD

*Atlantis* adds yet another interesting dimension to the popular colonial figure of John Galt.

Dr. T. Berto
School of English and Theatre Studies
University of Guelph, Ontario, Canada

## Works Cited

Fanon, Frantz. *Black Skin, White Masks*. New York: Grove Press, 2008.

Fanon, Frantz. *The Wretched of the Earth*. New York: Grove Press, 1963.

Freytag, Gustav. "Die Technik des Dramas." *Gustav Freytag. Dramatische Werke. Technik des Dramas. H. Fikentscher. o.J. Hirzel:* 1872 (2003).

Galt, John. "The Apostate; Or, Atlantis Destroyed." *New British Theatre* 1814 (Number 12, Volume 3; Pp. 305-345).

Silverman, David J. "Indians, Missionaries, and Religious Translation: Creating Wampanoag Christianity in Seventeenth-Century Martha's Vineyard," *William and Mary Quarterly*, 3rd series, LXII, no. 2 (April 2005).

Stanley, Brian. *The Bible and the Flag: Protestant Missions and British Imperialism in the Nineteenth and Twentieth Centuries*. Leicester, England: Apollos, 1990.

# INTRODUCTION

**David J. Knight**

I have copy-edited John Galt's five-act tragedy *The Apostate; Or, Atlantis Destroyed* from its 1814 appearance in the *New British Theatre* (Number 12, Volume 3; Pp. 305-345), a publication Galt was involved with.[1] The anonymous "Remarks on The Apostate" that appeared following the 1814 play (Pp. 346-348) are included here.

This is then followed by my copy-edit of John Galt's *The New Atlantis; An American Legend* from its 1831 appearance in *Friendship's Offering: A Literary Album, and Christmas and New Year's Present* (Smith, Elder; Pp. 217-229).[2]

It is interesting that this volume of *Friendship's Offering* also includes *The Captive*, by Susanna Strickland (later, and better known as, Susanna Moodie) (Pp. 184-186). I have included this eight-verse poem here. Susanna is best known as the younger sister of Agnes Strickland, Jane Margaret Strickland, and Catherine Parr Traill. She was also the sister of Samuel Strickland, who worked for John Galt in Guelph. Susanna wrote *The Captive* shortly before marrying John Moodie on 4 April, 1831, and a year before emigrating to Upper Canada. Galt's *The Apostate; Or, Atlantis Destroyed* was published over a decade before his travels to Canada, whereas his *The New Atlantis* is written from personal experience following his official role

---

[1] In Galt's *Autobiography* (Volume 1, 1833; Pp. 263-268) he outlines his involvement with the short-lived *Rejected Theatre*, which he worked on with Henry Colburn (1784-1855), a British publisher more notable for having published periodicals and works such as the *Literary Gazette* (as of 1817) and *Pepys's Diary* in 1825. Colburn changed the title of *Rejected Theatre* to the *New British Theatre*. This included "a selection of original dramas, not yet acted; some of which have been offered for representation, but not accepted: with critical remarks by the editor." The anonymous "remarks" on *The Apostate* are by Colburn.

[2] This was published in London by Smith, Elder & Co., 65, Cornhill, and printed by Littlewood & Co., Old Bailey.

with the Canada Company and foundation of Guelph on St. George's Day (April 23$^{rd}$, 1827. Strickland's *The Captive* was written immediately before her emigration. After returning to England (arriving May 20$^{th}$, 1829), Galt was imprisoned for several months for failure to pay his son's school fees. He "wrote himself out of jail" by putting to use his Canadian experiences. Galt's novels *Lawrie Todd* (1830), *Bogle Corbet* (1831), and his *Autobiography* (1833) were the works that established his stature as a New World author.

Galt's *Introduction* to *The New Atlantis* concerns observations of North American archaeological sites. He comments on ancient cities "beyond the Allegany mountains" and "in the regions of Canada to the north-west of the St. Lawrence." His identification of artifacts that resemble "Etruscan" urns is also found in his first letter from Guelph in 1827.[3]

The details of aboriginal culture in Galt's *The Apostate; Or, Atlantis Destroyed* were apparently (as mentioned by Colburn in his remarks to this play) communicated to him by a British traveller who spent a season hunting near Philadelphia, with the original occupants of the area, the Lenape (Delaware) Indians in the neighbourhood of their major village Shackamaxon.

By the mid-18$^{th}$ century, the Lenape (Delaware Indians) were pushed west from Pennsylvania by English-led settlers flowing into the colony. The Lenape were given permission by the Wyandot to settle in the Ohio country. One of their settlements was Maguck, built by 1750 on the banks of the Scioto River. Modern Circleville was built on the north of this site in 1810. Circleville derives its name from the circular portion of what is now known to have been a large Hopewell culture earthwork – the Hopewell tradition flourished up to A.D. 500. The Hopewell circles were documented by Caleb At-

---

[3]In the first letter from Guelph (dated August 1$^{st}$, 1827), John Galt wrote to his *Blackwood's Magazine* colleague Dr. David Moir in Musselburgh, including the anecdote: "By the way, in clearing for a quarry we discovered a neat formed niche in the rock, with a vase like an Etruscan in it, filled with dust and ashes – unfortunately it was broken by one of the workmen" (Bruce and Scott 125). Leanne Piper identifies this first quarry as located near the former Allan's Mill (personal communication; January 2017).

water and published by him in 1820: *Description of the Antiquities Discovered in the State of Ohio and Other Western States.*

In addition to descriptions of Lenape / Delaware culture that Galt was receiving from Philadelphia, he may later have included personally gathered information he encountered while in Canada West (Ontario). For instance, in *The New Atlantis*, Arak's trek to the west most likely incorporates a description of Niagara Falls.

The land upon which Galt founded Guelph was originally of the Chonnonton Nation, referred to by the French as *la Nation neutre* (Neutral Nation), who belonged to the Iroquoian Language group which included their neighbours, the Wyandot people, known also as the Wendat and Huron Nation, who referred to the Chonnonton rather impolitely as "Attawandaron," meaning "Those whose speech is awry," because they spoke a different dialect. By the 17th century the Attawandaron had about twenty-eight villages, with population concentrations on the Niagara Peninsula and near the present-day communities of Hamilton and Milton, Ontario. The 17th century seat of the Chief Souharissen was at Kandoucho, a now contested location (possibly near present-day Brantford, Ontario). In about 1650, the Iroquois declared war on the Attawandaron, and by 1653 the people were practically annihilated, and their villages wiped out, including Kandoucho. By the time of Galt's arrival in the area almost two centuries later, any remaining cultural memory echoes that may have entered his *The New Atlantis* would presumably relate more to the prevailing population of Iroquoian peoples.

The maritime Nations who currently inhabit Canada's eastern seaboard, where both *The Apostate* and *The New Atlantis* are set, are the Algonquin Mi'kmaq (Miawpukek First Nations), Maliseet, the Labrador Inuit, Sheshatshiu Innu First Nation, and Mushua Innu First Nation. The now lost Beothuk culture were related to the Mi'kmaq, and migrated from Labrador to present-day Newfoundland in *circa* A.D. 1. Some of the last identified Beothuk were Demasduit and her husband Nonosbawsut, who died in March of 1819. Demasduit died January 8, 1820, six years after *The Apostate* was published. The last known living member of the Beothuk was the niece of Demasduit,

Shanawdithit,[4] who died of tuberculosis in St. John's, Newfoundland, on June 6, 1829. There is an enticing possibility that an echo of Beothuk custom is present in Galt's *The Apostate*.

Galt's choice of character names is interesting; Orooko, in *The Apostate*, and Oroon in *The New Atlantis* may relate to Aphra Behn's 1688 short fictional account *Oroonoko: Or, The Royal Slave. A True History*. Arak can be traced to place-names in Iran, Syria, Algeria, and the alcoholic beverage of the Eastern Mediterranean and North Africa.[5] The name Icab may be a memory of the Hebraic Ichabod, brother of Ahitub (Books of Samuel), but perhaps more likely an echo of Ichabod Crane, the protagonist in Washington Irving's *The Legend of Sleepy Hollow* (1820). The name Idda, in *The Apostate*, may be a borrowing from *Idda of Tokenburg*.[6] The name Arutha may be a reworking of Ruth the Moabite in the *Book of Ruth* of the Hebrew Bible. Atlanthus is an obvious Latinized alternate to Atlantis. The use of Levantine and North African names, misapplied onto North American aboriginal peoples, was perhaps Galt's attempt to convey a sense of exotic otherness and foreign mystery to the 1814 and 1831 English readership.

John Galt's dramatic and prose version focus on much older tales of Atlantis and the conflict between aboriginal culture and the newly imported, colonial ideologies. The main influences on Galt's choice of Atlantis as a catalyst for his renderings include Plato, More and Bacon. Sir Thomas More's fictional *Utopia* (16th Century) was inspired by Plato's Atlantis and travellers accounts of the Americas, his idealistic vision established a connection between the Americas and Utopian societies, a theme which was further solidified by Sir Francis Bacon in *The New Atlantis* (c. 1623). Galt's *The New Atlantis* proves to be dystopian and a blight to the original nations of the Americas. In 1818, Jeremy Bentham originally proposed cacotopia

---

[4] Also noted as Shawnadithititis, Shawnawdithit, Nancy April, and Nancy Shanawdithit.

[5] The word arak derives from the Arabic 'araq, meaning "sweat."

[6] *Idda of Tokenburg; Or, the Force of Jealousy*, "Translated from the German of Augustus Lafontaine," was printed in *The Lady's Magazine, Or Entertaining Companion for the Fair Sex: Appropriate Solely to Their Use and Amusement* (Baldwin, Cradock & Joy; 1801), Volume 32, Pp. 28-35.

# INTRODUCTION

"As a match for utopia...the imagined seat of the worst government" (*Plan of Parliamentary Reform, in the form of a catechism*). Galt's subtitle, *An American Legend*, also may relate to Washington Irving's earlier work, and the early 19th century vogue for writing legends.

I believe that publishing a new edition of *The Apostate* and *The New Atlantis* demonstrates that John Galt, in an official position with the Canada Company, and therefore at the forefront of colonisation, was, as a writer and artist, a Humanist who openly questioned the underlying problems of Colonialism. His demonstrated affinity with the tragedy of clashing cultures makes him an important figure not to be painted with one broad brushstroke within the pertinent discourse of reconciliation. Galt was bravely challenging Colonialism in the very midst of its heyday, and if these writings of his are now reconsidered in this light, his warnings of the demise of the First Nations may be seen as prophetic.

DAVID J. KNIGHT
General Editor – Vocamus Editions
Guelph, Ontario, Canada

## References

Bruce, G. and Scott, P. H.. "A Scottish Postbag: Eight Centuries of Scottish Letters." *The Saltire Society*, 2002.

# THE APOSTATE; OR, ATLANTIS DESTROYED

## Characters

**YAMOS**

King of Atlantis, converted to Christianity, and Founder of the City.

**OROOKO**

A Priest of the ancient religion of the Country, who has retired with a few followers into the woods.

**ARAK**

An Officer of the Palace, in love with MORA.

**SEBI**

An Elder of the tribes who constitute the people of Atlantis, and father of MORA.

**ANTONIO**

A European, saved from shipwreck by YAMOS, whom he has converted to Christianity, and instructed in the arts and polity of Europe.

**IDDA**

The wife of YAMOS, in love with ANTONIO.

**MORA**

The daughter of SEBI, betrothed to ARAK, but in love with ANTONIO.

Elders of the Tribes

# THE APOSTATE

Females attendant on IDDA

Atlantines

Priests and Officers of the Palace.

# ACT I, SCENE ONE

*A Forest with openings, which disclose vast mountains and
cataracts at a distance.*

ARAK: (*alone*) How holy is this calm magnificence
Of mountain, lake, and wood! The ceaseless blair
Of the hoarse cataracts, by distance soften'd,
Seems but the soothing lull of Nature's voice,
Charming all thought into tranquillity. –
Here I will stop till old Orooko come,
Nor on the simple worshippers intrude,
Who still with him refuse the Christian faith,
And 'mid these scenes of solemn loneliness,
With aimless rites and ineffectual prayer,
Adore the fancied powers, our nation served,
Till good Antonio from the ocean waves
Was sent by Heaven, to teach the truth divine.

*Enter OROOKO.*

OROOKO: Who art thou, that within these hallow'd shades
Presum'st in that apostate garb to enter?

ARAK: Do you not know me?

OROOKO: Arak! is it thee?
Nay, no embrace, – Thou hast the Gods forsaken,
And I their priest must never more again
Receive thee to these arms, nor ever raise
My hands above thee, to implore their blessing. –
O ye unknown dread and beneficent!
Whose genial power all artless creatures praise,

Pardon these tears, forgive my weak old heart,
That would forget this hapless young man's sin,
And still receive him, as your gracious spirit
Taught me to look upon all human kind. –
Oh, then I knew not that such things could be
As man presuming to select his God. –
Yet, Arak, if in penitence you come,
Come to my heart, and with most joyful tears
I'll bathe thy forehead, and absolve thy sin.

ARAK: I bring a message from the king to you.

OROOKO: What would he now with me. Oh, he might spare
The little remnant I have left of life,
To the deserted worship of the Gods, –
His country's Gods, – Those ever-bounteous powers,
That blest his fathers from the first of time,
Nor ever once upon our happy tribes
Sent civil discord, till that fatal hour,
When on our coast the curs'd Antonio came,
Like something horrible cast from the sea,
To mar, with his perplexing arts and faith,
Our sacred rites and old simplicity.

ARAK: Alas, Orooko, you will not discern
The good, the blessing in Antonio given.

OROOKO: Within the bowers of these far-spreading woods,
We happy dwelt, and with the morning light
Our song as cheerful as the grateful birds
Rose to the powers that bless'd us – all the day
The active chace gave energy to health,
And when at night, our frugal meal dispatch'd,
We stretch'd ourselves beneath the fragrant boughs,
We fear'd no danger in the form of man,
For we had nothing then that could be stolen.
Spirit of Nature, did my tongue say nothing? –

Yes, we had happiness, and that sweet ease –
And the sea outcast has purloin'd them all.

60 ARAK: But he has given us better, and tenfold –
Taught us to rear the safe and shelt'ring shed,
The woes that wait on perjury and crimes,
And the rich promise of a second life,
A glorious morning to the night of death. –
–But the king summons you.

OROOKO: What does he want?
I cannot aid him in his new designs –
My heart grows sad whene'er by chance afar
My wand'ring eyes see, through the opening woods,
70 His rising town; and sad presages come,
Lest the dread Gods, whose secret throne of fires,
Deep in the hollow of the mountain glows,
Will burst the earth, and sweep in floods of flame
Th' apostates and their perishable homes. –
But what can Yamos now require of me?
O he was once the sunshine of my soul,
And never, never, did prolific Nature
A being fashion in the human form
So good, so kind, so modest, and so brave. –
80 Methinks I could have pardon'd all the tribes,
Had they rais'd altars to adore that youth,
For then they had but worshipped in him
Th' embodied excellence of all that lives.
Alas! that goodness has but caus'd this ill,
And but for it the fraudulent Antonio
Had been thrown back into the hungry sea,
When first he dared to slight our ancient rites –
But grief bewilders me – I lose myself –
Why does the king require me in Atlantis?

90 ARAK: The queen of late, drooping forgoes his love,
And he desires that with your speediest skill
You would restore to him her wonted kindness.

# THE APOSTATE

OROOK: Though she too is apostate, I will go. –
Lead on, I'll follow: never, but to take
Some gentle essence of appeasing herbs,
To quiet sorrow, or extinguish pain,
Shall e'er my feet towards your city tend.

*Exeunt.*

# ACT I, SCENE TWO

*An apartment in the Palace of* YAMOS.
YAMOS *and* ANTONIO.

YAMOS: Thrice have the trees renew'd and shed their leaves,
And the fourth fruit hangs blushing on the bough,
Since thou, Antonio, child of Providence,
Wast on our shore, snatch'd from the greedy waves
To bless our wilds and world undivulg'd
To thy far countrymen, who dwell beyond
The rising sun. O ever since that hour,
How rich in knowledge hast thou made us all!
Teaching our docile youth the arts of peace;
The all-cementing harmony of law,
And like the new moon, out of darkness born,
Still more and more, to the full round of light,
Brightening our souls, though with the dim reflex
Of that eternal truth, which in thy land
Sheds the warm mid-day beam – In all this time,
With constant wisdom ever blessing us,
Thou hast thyself been still alone unblest.

ANTONIO: Most gracious Yamos, in what I have done
I feel my happiness a rich reward,
And the proud honors which the good unborn
Will pay my name, already I foretaste. –
The time will come, when from the Eastern world,
With spreading sail, some daring mariner
Will this way steer, then all these unknown scenes
Of inland seas and forests infinite
Shall be reveal'd. Oft, sir, as I have told,
Their winged vessels would the way explore,

And that in which I 'scap'd the waves to you,
Was sent in quest of this great continent,
Of which some dark report had long prevail'd: –
And when they come and find the arts of Europe
In sweet communion with the Christian faith,
130    My name shall rise to an equality
With that of Cadmus or of Bacchus,[1] those
Who in the elder time brought westward truth.

YAMOS: But wherefore wilt thou not be one of us –
Our nation shall to thy posterity
Give higher honors than to all our kings.
I pray thee, friend – or rather let me call thee
Creative genius of our rising world,
Consent to what we ask – the gentle Mora,
The daughter of the venerable Sebi,
140    Has long the influence of thy virtues felt –
Felt as the rose-bud feels the solar beam,
And to their brightness would unfold her breast. –
You seem perplex'd, why should my words disturb you?
Why do you sigh and look like one that heard
Unhappy tidings – tell me why is this?

ANTONIO: My heart is grateful to your Majesty,
But in the rearing of your infant state
I find abundant blessing – Did I yield
To soft endearments, my ennobling aims
150    Might sink abortive, and entail but woe.

YAMOS: Thou hast, Antonio, yet but given precept,
Give us example too, that we may see
By thy bright practice how to guide ourselves.
The rights of fathers, husbands, sons, and men,
Thou hast prescrib'd to us. Take now a wife,

---

[1]Cadmus was a Phoenician Prince (brother to Europa) who founded and became King of Thebes. Bacchus is the Roman equivalent of Dionysus, the Greek god of wine-making and theatre.

And by thy actions in the wedded state,
Show us in what our customs need example.

ANTONIO: There is a beauty, sir, in principles,
Which those who most in theory revere,
160    Cannot transfuse into their way of life.
I have denied myself connubial love,
Lest I should not in practice so conform
To the great precepts I aspire to teach.

YAMOS: I will no farther press this matter, friend:
I humbly own the grandeur of thy motive,
I do thee homage for't; but while you thus
Appear a doubting, conscious, erring man,
Such virtue makes you glorious as a God.

*Exit the king.*

ANTONIO: O noble being, how art thou deceiv'd;
170    How black and horrible methinks I show
Beside the lustre of thy purer nature!
Thou dost sustain me, Yamos, in thy love,
As the new moon in its first hoop of brightness,
Holds in embrace the dark and rayless old.

*Exit.*

# ACT I, SCENE THREE

*Another Apartment.*
YAMOS *and* IDDA.

YAMOS: Alas, dear Idda, wherefore would'st thou shun me?
The time was once that I was all to thee –
The blossom breathing to the mid-day sun,
Its bosom's fragrance, never was more faithful
Than thy sweet love, the fragrance of the heart,
Was wont to meet me; but how art thou chang'd!
Ah me, how chang'd! looking askance upon me,
As at some hateful reptile that you fear'd –
And yet to thee I am entirely love.

IDDA: I know not, Yamos, why I should be thus, –
I would be to thee what I was before,
But some foul vapor hath beset my brain,
And stain'd the wonted substance of my thoughts.

YAMOS: Since good Antonio has not yet been able
To turn again thy far-reverted love
Back to its proper course; but still the more
This woeful change works to increas'd dislike,
I have sent Arak to the old Orooko,
To bring him with his genial simples here,
That we may try their power.

IDDA: I'll none of them.
Leave where he lives that petulant old man;
What would he here, but fret, as he was wont,
Against Antonio, and with searching eyes
Make still more irksome my unquiet heart.

YAMOS: Does he too, Idda, grow displeasing to thee?
Once that old man was to thee as a God;
And God-like was his fault, for it was kindness.

IDDA: But is he not Antonio's enemy?

YAMOS: He has refused to take the Christian faith -
But there's no enmity in his kind nature.
I'd think as soon Antonio bad and false,
As I could think Orooko would molest.

IDDA: But wherefore bring him here? – I need him not,
And he may vex Antonio with his prying.

YAMOS: Unhappy Idda, to what strange conceits
Thy thoughts and fancies turn. Why should he pry?
Nor from the freedom of a good old man
Can there be aught Antonio would conceal.
But thou art ill at ease; fair Mora droops,
And all our wonted medicines have fail'd.
Alas, poor Mora! solitary – still
With hopeless wishes must she ever pine.
Antonio has rejected her.

IDDA: Rejected!

YAMOS: He will not marry; constant to the bent
Of the great purpose that exalts his mind
Above our nature, he will never join
His fate to any woman's.

IDDA: Did you ask?

YAMOS: Even now I did.

IDDA: And wherefore did you that?

YAMOS: Can it offend you, Idda, that I sought
To make him happy, who has blest my people?

IDDA: Had you no other motive?

230      YAMOS: Ah what other?

IDDA: But he rejected her, and will not marry?

YAMOS: Why should that lighten up your eyes with joy?
When you might grieve to think ill-fated Mora
Must hopeless sigh in unrequited love.

IDDA: Love! said you love! (*aside.*) Ah now I know the cause
Of her averse and fearful diffidence.

YAMOS: My dearest Idda, my once gentle Idda,
Why should this news such angry looks excite.
Yes, Mora loves the excellent Antonio.

240      IDDA: O not to love him were almost a sin –
But my fit comes – O Yamos, o'er my head
Methinks some hideous and unholy thing
Hath perch'd itself, and feeds upon my brain –
I would I were not what I am, or could
Again the fondness of thy love return.

*Exeunt.*

# ACT II, SCENE ONE

*A Portico.*
YAMOS, OROOKO, &c.

YAMOS: Welcome, Orooko, give me yet thy hand;
Come, be not sad, but make our meeting joyous.
You were to me a loving father once,
And I am still to you a faithful son.

250     OROOKO: I feel towards you as I always felt,
But here are sights afflicting to my eyes,
Turning the pleasure of this hour to woe.

YAMOS: To me, to all, your re-appearance here,
Is cheerful as the sunbeams after night.

OROOKO: And night it has been, Yamos, since we parted;
A night of dreams, whose phantoms still deceive,
O let me hope that thou wilt 'waken from them.

YAMOS: And yet these gorgeous objects rising round,
The tow'ring city, and these royal ensigns
260     Of arts and polity, should teach my friend,
All is not fantasy. – The sleep was yours.
Like the sun-loving bird that sleeps in winter,
And wak'ning in the spring, finds Nature new;
Cover'd with blossoms and resounding songs,
You come among us wond'ring at the change.

OROOKO: The arts, the ornaments which you admire,
Are as the speckles and the glittering eye
Of the fell snake, and these increasing sounds,

The stir of labor in your guilty town,
But as the rattle that announces death.

YAMOS: Is there then nothing that can please your eye
In all this new magnificence?

OROOKO: No, nothing.

YAMOS: Would you we should resign the social arts –
The various pleasures industry makes ours,
And sink into barbarity again.

OROOKO: I wish you only to cast off the vices,
Which with these gaudy garments you put on.
The virtues need no robes, they ever move
In healthy vigor, naked like your sires.
But these gay trappings of civilization
Are but the covers of offensive sores. –
As I came sadly to this spacious dwelling,
Two stately edifices met my view; –
One was too great, too lofty as I thought
For any use of man; the other seem'd
Too closely strong, even for the fiercest beasts.
What are they, sir?

YAMOS: One is a temple hallow'd,
Open and free for our religious rites.

OROOKO: What! does the God, the stranger has reveal'd,
Live like a creature local and limited.

YAMOS: The God we worship is the God of Nature,
The spirit of the ocean and the earth!

OROOKO: Then wherefore have you built to him a house,
When the whole universe is full of him?
In light and blossoms, and melodious sounds,
We know his beauty; in the fruits and sleep,

16

And in the gladness of the blameless breast,
300    We feel his bounty and enjoy his care;
The skies so vast and inaccessible,
With their infinitude of stars attest
To us his greatness; in the strength of hills,
The deep foundations of the steadfast earth
And the long fetching of his breath in tempests,
We own his mighty power; and when we question
Why we do live and all this world should be,
We recognise his undiscover'd Nature.
Is it to HIM that you have built a house?

310    YAMOS: You will but see our works in your own way;
We have not rear'd the church for his abode,
But as a place in which we may remember
That he exists, and should be there adored.

OROOKO: Does then your knowledge, your civilization,
Tend to make you forget him? Royal Yamos,
Our fathers never dreaded such a chance.
They heard him in the roaring of the waves;
They trembled at his anger in the thunder,
They fear'd the flapping of his wings in storms;
320    They hail'd his smiling in the dawn of morn;
They felt his kindness in the warmth of day,
And like tired children in their mother's lap,
They trusted to him in the nightly sleep.
O he was every-where and they were with him.
But for what purpose is your other fabric?

YAMOS: It is a prison, an appointed lodge,
For such as wrongful injure one another.

OROOKO: Stop, Yamos, stop. O swift retrace your steps,
To that simplicity that once was yours.
330    Already lo, your new-found arts require
Inventions to remind you of the God.

Already they have taught you to prepare
Abodes for men, men worse than savage beasts;
If in a few short moons all these are needful,
Think what shall rise when future ages come.
If there are men that must be shut in dungeons,
The bad in time may overtop the good,
And make them to their wicked purposes
Offer themselves in hideous sacrifice.

340      YAMOS: I will no longer now debate with you.
Come in and see the Queen, and if you can,
Restore her errant love again to me.

*Exeunt.*

# ACT II, SCENE TWO

*An Apartment.*
ARAK *and* MORA

ARAK: Why will you, Mora, ever thus avoid me,
Why ever thus averted turn your eyes?
O look upon me; let me see again,
That gracious loveliness which won my heart,
But still, O still, must I in vain address you,
Your cold and alter'd looks in vain deplore?

MORA: Leave me, good Arak, leave me to myself,
I would I were deserving of thy love.

ARAK: Alas, what frenzies now are rife among us!
Yamos bewails his consort's faded love,
And must I, Mora, also mourn for thine?

MORA: It had been better, had we never known
These gay and festal arts Antonio teaches,
Than thus to feel all ties of truth relax'd.
Surely from them this sad perversion springs!

ARAK: O say not so, believe not so, dear maid;
Say rather he has taught us to cast off
Our savage nature, and with purer thoughts
So temper'd and refin'd our base desires
That we are rais'd into a nobler state.
Alas, perchance the passion of my heart,
Is but some dross of my barbarity,
Not yet remov'd. Ah it appears to thee
So gross and foul, that thou hast turn'd away,

Tir'd of my fondness, and with royal Idda
Delighted shar'st his ever-varying wisdom.

MORA: O spare me, Arak, spare me, noble youth!

370    ARAK: Ha! why is this? O wherefore do you weep?

MORA: Most true it is that I have been too oft
A happy listener to Antonio's voice.

ARAK: And mine no more is pleasant to your ear.

MORA: But grieve not, Arak. I am innocent.

ARAK: Innocent! could you have e'er been guilty?
Guilty! of what! you are not yet my wife,
And if your heart be chang'd, though I must mourn,
Alas, must languish without hope of cure,
Why should the change be link'd to thoughts of guilt?
380    No, Mora, no. I long have fear'd this truth:
Antonio's virtues, like the solar beams
Which by their brightness quench the dim dull hearth,
Have all thy former love for me extinguish'd.
But gentle maid, to me for ever dear,
I will no more molest thee with thy suit.
But speedily with all my earnest thoughts
Devise the means to make thee blest with him.

MORA: O Arak, Arak, you know not the man.

*Exeunt.*

# ACT II, SCENE THREE

*Another Apartment.*
OROOKO, YAMOS *and* IDDA

OROOKO: Why do you chide your lord, why is his love
Thus bitterly repell'd?

YAMOS: 'Tis her disease;
Be not, Orooko, wroth with her, but try
Some kind appeasing med'cine to allay
This fretful ecstasy of peevish thought.

IDDA: I am not ill, old man, trouble me not.
I want no med'cines, but the cooling charm
Of your desir'd absence. Give it me?

OROOKO: I do not think you ill of malady,
But some infection taints the conscious mind.
What fatal wrong have you done to your lord,
That you look on him with such eyes of hate,
While love and tenderness so melts in him?

YAMOS: All things, Orooko, seem to thee revers'd.

OROOKO: 'Tis meet I should converse with her alone.

YAMOS: Bear with him, Idda, let him have his way,
He is a man full of most bounteous feeling,
And comes obedient – not to my command,
But to the gentle spirit of himself
To cure your bosom's pain. I beg, Orooko,
That you will mercifully hear her chidings,
Think what she once was to me, loving kind;

O this dire change but serves to make her dearer.
Yes, the remembrance of our former love
Stands in bright contrast to the void of loss,
Making the beauteous and delightful past,
Compar'd with the unhappy vacant present,
Like the sad lesson of a rosy child
That smiling gambols round a yawning grave.
Be kindly in your speech – and if her thoughts
420   Be touch'd with aught that hath perplex'd their course,
In pitying care the remedy apply

*Exit* YAMOS.

IDDA: Well, Sir, what would you?

OROOKO: How! so soon at ease?
Then you do fear the King as well as hate him?
What is the wrong that you have done to him?
That you should dread his sight, and in his presence
Be weak and trembling, looking with such eyes
Upon that goodly and most gracious man,
As if he were some creature venomous?
430   What is the cause?

IDDA: Came you not here to find it?

OROOKO: Such maladies as yours were never known,
When all were true to their forefathers' virtues,
Therefore the cause – Ay, lady, mark my words,
The cause must come from this new state of things.
Why do you look at me in such amaze?
Then it is true, and your apostasy
Has changed the frame and temper of your heart.
O ere more horror falls in curses on you,
440   Abjure the subtile stranger's unblest rites;
And on the mountain's top, that altar rais'd,
By all-seen Nature to the all-felt God,
Lift thy pale hands and deprecate thy doom.

What! do you smile, and scornfully at this –
The mind has then no part in your disease –
You mock my piety, and when I bid
You turn repentant from the stranger's Gods,
You do not hear me as a proselyte,
But with the heartless and contemptuous scorn
450 Of one that reverenc'd not any God.

IDDA: I wonder much that you, so wise reputed,
Should waste your ineffectual breath on me.

OROOKO: (*aside*) They have built dungeons for those that do
          ill –
This woman must be one that has done ill,
For she no longer hath that modesty
With which our faithful mothers heard reproof.
Your royal husband called me from the woods,
With herbs and simples to relieve your ail;
But the disease is far beyond the search
460 Of all the inquisition of my skill,
And I may sorrowing to the woods return.

*Exeunt.*

# ACT II, SCENE FOUR

*A Garden.*
ARAK *and* ANTONIO

ARAK: That the fair Mora loves you tenderly,
And has for you forgone her love to me,
I doubt no more, nor can I blame the change,
When I contrast my naked ignorance,
With that rich-crown'd, that flowing vestured knowledge,
Which makes you ever to my wond'ring eyes,
Appear the sovereign wisdom of all times.
But while my tongue thus says, what I should say,
470     My heart, alas, still in its savage grossness,
Yearns at the sacrifice and speaks in tears.

ANTONIO: No: generous Arak, thy true heart is right,
And 'tis thy judgment that mistakes in this.
I am not worthy of fair Mora's love,
Reclaim her yet, re-win her for thyself,
Would she were worthy thee, and I like thee,
Could merit her by so resigning her.

ARAK: O hapless Mora, fated like thy lover,
To feel the anguish of rejected passion! –
480     Have you no charm that you can give to me,
To lure her truant heart to its first love?
Or some endearing cordial for yourself,
To make you see her with fond eyes like mine?
But see, Orooko comes. If he can turn
The Queen's affection to her lord again,
Perchance his skill may Mora's too reclaim.

ANTONIO: (*aside*) O Heavens, what horror am I doom'd to
    suffer?

        ARAK *during this soliloquy has advanced towards*
OROOKO.

How the pure fancies of this guileless race
Make the foul odium of my guilt appear!
490    They look on me as on the orb of day;
O little think they that the light they worship
Gleams but from dead and guilty rottenness,
Compar'd to which they are themselves Heaven's stars.

        *Enter* OROOKO, *and* ARAK *returns.*

OROOKO: Unhappy Arak! I will speak to him.

ANTONIO: (*to* OROOKO) Have you been able to relieve the
    Queen?

OROOKO: (*to* ANTONIO) You only can do that, – why do you
    start?
The ill that taints her bosom came by you –
And you should, Sir, in bringing such disease,
Have brought with it the needful antidote.
500    Are such distempers common in your country?

ANTONIO: I fear they are.

OROOKO: The gentle Mora too,
Arak's betroth'd, has caught the same infection;
Sir, you seem greatly mov'd. I mean no harm,
I only grieve that with the arts you teach,
Such fearful and appalling reprobation,
Should thus destroy the ties of faithful love.

ARAK: But Mora is not, like her royal Mistress,
Afraid and angry when I speak to her.
510    She owns her love and treats me as a brother.

OROOKO: Show owns her love! what love?

ARAK: Love for Antonio!

ANTONIO: (*aside*) Ha! he has caught the truth!

ARAK: What means this?

OROOKO: Leave us, dear Arak – leave us for a while.

*Exit* ARAK.

Stay, Sir, you must remain, a word, a word.
The giant bark that brought you to our coast
Seem'd as it welter'd on the surfy shore,
Some monstrous thing presaging woe to us.
520  From all the haunts of all our woody land,
Successive came our wand'ring tribes, to see
The awful sight. And with compassion mov'd
Our youthful monarch, Yamos, took thy hand
And plac'd thee by himself, an honor'd guest.
At that dire hour your dreadful work began.
You taught us arts – divided us in bands,
These for the chace, and those to seed the soil,
And when your tongue had learnt our simple speech,
You spoke of life and worlds beyond the stars,
530  And call'd our ancient rites of gratitude,
To the great Spirit – aimless superstition.

ANTONIO: In doing so, I know that I did well.

OROOKO: The proof of that must show in the effect.
But I proceed – Dissensions rose among us –
Your altars prosper'd, while with hapless me
A few undaunted faithful chose the woods.
Here, here enchanted by your seeming wisdom,
Thousands on thousands swarm'd to raise the town,
And it was rais'd. For this eternal temple,

540 High in whose measureless concave the sun
A lamp of everlasting splendor shines,
You have th' Apostates from their father's God,
Led to a mansion built by their own hands,
And made them kneel before such feeble emblems,
As the soft-breathing of a bird, might quench;
And you have dungeons rear'd.

ANTONIO: O let me fly –

OROOKO: Fly! whither. No. – You shall hear all your works,
Now answer me. – The gentle Mora loves you, –
550 For you her heart has turn'd from gen'rous Arak,
And yet she sees him with nor hate, nor fear –
Thy pallid visage [1] tells me all I ask. –
Go to thy temples, prisons, knowledge, arts,
And find some means to purge our tainted tribes,
From these new sins that thou hast brought with them.

---

[1] A poetic form of "paleface," although ascribed as an ethnic slur of white people by some Native Americans, Galt's version here, in 1814, may either be his own invention or his translation of the slur.

# ACT III, SCENE ONE

*A Vestibule.*
OROOKO, SEBI *and* ARAK.

OROOKO. Go, summon without preface or delay,
The honor'd elders of the tribes to meet.

SEBI: They hold the magistracy of the town.

OROOKO: No matter, go. Tell them I would impart
Things of most high concernment to us all.
They were not wont in the old better time,
To wait for dues of ceremonious state.

*Exit* SEBI.

Who is with Yamos? who is with the King?

ARAK: He is alone.

OROOKO: What you here, Arak! Arak?

ARAK: Ah me, Sir, what has chanced? (*aside*) He is perplex'd,
His thoughts coil inward, and his eyes are fierce,
As the fell snake's when it unfolds itself
To spring upon its victim.

OROOKO: Where is the stranger?

ARAK: Antonio?

OROOKO: Where has he fled?

ARAK: How fled?
I saw him scarce a hundred breathings since,
Enter the portal of the Queen's apartment.

*Exit* OROOKO.

Surely some hideous madness touches all,
For thoughts, and fears impossible, appal me,
And when I told him where Antonio was,
He shriek'd as if he had a serpent trod.

*Exit.*

# ACT III, SCENE TWO

*An apartment and Couch. – music without.*
YAMOS *and* Attendants.

580     YAMOS: Bid the musicians cease. Let them forebear.
The soft melodious sadness of their song
Awakens in me but unhappy thoughts. –
Methinks the ghosts of all my ancestors,
Hover around me, and in piteous silence,
Look on my grieved and melancholy mind.
O sure some dreadful woe unseen impends
That thus my heart feels cold as kneaded clay.
Send for Antonio to me.

1ˢᵗ ATTENDANT: He is here.

*Enter* ANTONIO.

590     YAMOS: Art thou too sad, my friend, pray thee draw near,
Sit here by me, I would converse awhile,
To learn why thus my anxious spirit pines,
And questions oft the use of all our labors?

ANTONIO: Such weary thoughts, sir, frequently arise,
When the exhausted spirit needs repose.
They are the dreams of reason, and molest,
Like the night visions, only while they last.[1]

YAMOS: And shall I wake from this unhappiness;
Shall my lov'd Idda chearfully awake?

---

[1] Apparently a reference to Francisco Goya's *circa* 1799 etching *The Sleep of Reason Produces Monsters* (*El sueño de la razón produce monstruos*).

And take me back with those endearing arms
With which she press'd me to her virgin breast?
Alas, you sigh – there is no hope of that.

*Enter* OROOKO.

How now, Orooko, why these looks of rage;
What new discov'ry in the town alarms?

OROOKO: Stranger, avaunt.

YAMOS: What change is this, Antonio?

OROOKO: He shall not stay, let him at once retire!

YAMOS: Treason, Guards, ho! Dost thou menace, old man?
What hast thou done, that thou dar'st thus insult
Our royal presence with this fierce demeanour.
Antonio, fear him not. I will protect thee.
Though mutiny and rash rebellion rise,
By his incitement. I am still thy friend.
You weep and tremble – weeps Orooko too?
Friends, why is this?

OROOKO: Let him retire. Retire.

*Exit* ANTONIO.

YAMOS: Now he is gone, what would you say to me?

OROOKO: The thunder's voice heard in the summer's calm,
Nor the great Spirit's when he heaves the woods,
In wilder billows than the roaring ocean,
Speaks no such horror, as I must unfold.

YAMOS: Orooko, tell me, is my Idda dead?

OROOKO: Curses descend on her. Let fury come,
And wide and numberless as all the leaves,
That the winds scatter when the forests fade,
Disperse the ashes of her guilty form.

YAMOS: Thou art not mad, Orooko? yet thou speak'st
More frantic ecstasy than the loose wrack,
Of scatter'd thought, in the disorder'd mind
630    Hath ever yet assum'd.

OROOKO: The Queen is false.

YAMOS: False, False? Repeat what thou hast said – the word.
My ears ring fearfully – repeat the word. –

OROOKO: False with Antonio.

YAMOS: Hoary liar, ha!

*strikes him down.*

OROOKO: (*on the ground.*)
Gods of his fathers, take my thanks for this.
Now must the noble soul of Yamos feel,
By this dishonor he has done himself
640    In striking me, his own, his father's friend!
What shame and woe springs from Antonio's guile.

YAMOS: Th' infection works, in every joint I feel
The withering horror seizing on my strength.
It was delirium! and I heard it not.
No one did say to me my wife was false –
Antonio! O to what wicked thoughts
The idle fancy will betake itself!
While the musicians sang, I closed my eyes,
Strange fears oppress'd me. I would see Antonio, –
650    He came and he was sad. Orooko came –
Is that Orooko on the ground before me?

OROOKO: (*rising.*)
Distraction kindles in him, help, O help! –

YAMOS: Hush, hush, we will be calm, we will be calm.

*They sit down.*

Come, sit thee down – we will discourse of this –
And first I will relate my dream to thee –
Antonio – no, he is not. – O my heart,
It swells to thrice three hearts, and stops my breath.
Once I did think he fondly look'd at her,

660  And she responded with familiar smiles,
Such as no wife may blamelessly express. –
And when I chid her for't, that hate began,
Which no imploring love of mine could alter,
No tend'rest grief since that dire hour appease.

OROOKO: Did you observe their love?

YAMOS: What love? what love?
I but beheld a free unseemly glance.
What have you seen?

OROOKO: Alas, dear noble Yamos,

670  Such looks unchaste were never known before.

YAMOS: Ha! is it for that, you have so tortur'd me.
And for your worship and availless rites
Would tempt me thus to sacrifice my friend.
Away, old man – back to thy wilds again;
Provoke me not with guilty imputation,
To think as ill of thy respected self,
As thy fell bigotry would say of others.
What is this knowledge, that with painful throes
My mind would bring into the world of thought,

680  And on it, as a mother o'er her child,
All other things forsaking, fondly doat –

33

Suspicion! Suspicion! O forerunning shadow
Of coming woe – more hideous than the substance.
If this Antonio be the wretch you think;
If Idda be the victim of his guile;
What may ensue? – Nothing more ill than is!
And the good springing from Antonio's knowledge
Must still be good, let him be what he may.

OROOKO: How know you that?

690     YAMOS: I will endure no more;
If thus I listen to thy venomous tongue,
I shall believe the glorious sun himself
Black as eclipse – Away, away, and leave me.

*Exeunt.*

# ACT III, SCENE THREE

*Another Apartment.*
IDDA *and* MORA.

IDDA: Find me Antonio; bring him to me here:
For old Orooko thinks what he should not,
And we must turn the current of his thoughts. –
Why do you stand? Go, bring Antonio to me.

MORA: Forbear, I pray you – While Orooko's here,
Seek not that fatal man. O royal Idda,
700    Ere yet too late, if it be not too late,
Snatch your affections from this headlong stream;
It draws you swiftly to a deep perdition!

IDDA: I am not, Mora, to be told, your eyes
Betray the wishes of your throbbing heart
Towards Antonio. Pray thee, gentle maid,
Give me not reason to suspect thy truth,
By the great virtue which thy tongue affects.

MORA: O I am conscious of my erring nature,
My mind contemning what my heart desires;
710    But surely, surely, it becomes not you
To blame a fault that I have still restrain'd!

IDDA: Obey my orders.

MORA: Freely in all else.

IDDA: Do you refuse me then? – Ha! Arak here!

*Enter ARAK.*

Why come you here, sir, with such looks of terror?

ARAK: Where is Antonio?

IDDA: How! He is not here.

ARAK: Orooko, by his old prerogatives,
Convenes the magistrates, and they assemble:
I would Antonio were prepared for this;
Such convocation bodes to him no good.

MORA: Ah, royal Idda, do not doubt my faith.

ARAK: Is not Antonio here?

IDDA: What should he here?

ARAK: That were not fitting for me to inquire;
But if I saw him, and might speak to him,
Perhaps I could such signs of trouble tell,
That he might shun the danger they forewarn –
Stern thoughts have gain'd the solemn mastery
Of old Orooko's wonted gentleness.

IDDA: Go, seek Antonio then – Go, Mora, too:
Here I shall languish for your swift return.

*Exeunt* ARAK *and* MORA.

My heart shrinks in me, and I tremble all,
Like one that has pernicious berries ate,
And 'gins to feel the ill juice in her blood,
Clotting the pulses of the vital stream.

*Enter* ANTONIO.

ANTONIO: But for the woman's sympathetic lewdness
Stirring the vice in me that I had quell'd,
I might have left, in this new world, a name
To match the brightest of antiquity.

720

730

740

36

IDDA: Antonio!

ANTONIO: Ha! what would'st thou?

IDDA: Softly, hear me –

ANTONIO: No more, no more.

IDDA: Do you Orooko dread?

ANTONIO: We have together drank a fatal draught,
And now the poison burns straight on to death.

IDDA: Hear me, Antonio –

ANTONIO: Horror and Death
Have seiz'd upon me, and in folds of flame
The one envelopes my distracted soul,
While the cold other with his icy fang
Grasps me immoveably.

IDDA: Will you not answer?

ANTONIO: Well, what would you?

IDDA: Do you dread Orooko?

ANTONIO: I dread myself – O rather let me say
I have done that which I cannot undo,
And by the guilt made awful forfeiture
Of the high destiny that once was mine.
This having done, and from all honor driven,
I know not what extremity of guilt
My out-cast doom may draw me yet to do.

IDDA: Hush, hush; this fierce impassion'd rage repress –
Into my chamber, where we shall be safe.

ANTONIO: To hell at once! – O I already suffer
The torments of damnation in the thought
Of what I was, of what I might have been.

IDDA: We whirl in jeopardy; the tide of fate
770    May sweep us from the chance within our reach,
If we delay to catch.

ANTONIO: Then let us sink,
And time close over us as smooth and trackless
As the deep ocean o'er the bottom's sand.

IDDA: O it is true what our old warriors say;
The lofty mansion and the stately couch
Unnerve the body and impair the mind.
Thou hast not manhood in thee to endure
The test which our heroic youth were wont
780    To rise refulgent from – Adversity!
The worst that can ensue to both of us,
What is it but to die?

ANTONIO: The death of life,
The dagger, or the stake, appal not me.

IDDA: What then dismays you?

ANTONIO: Fame and honor lost.

IDDA: Were they not lost till old Orooko came?
Has his suspicion, which makes us unsafe,
Chang'd too the quality of our fond love?
790    Before this day you never own'd alarm;
But now when he menaces to destroy,
Behold, the memory of fame and honor
Comes like a ghost to frighten your repose.

ANTONIO: Yes, yes, from sleep – I am indeed awake!

IDDA: And being so, up and appear the man,
And show your brightening forehead to the storm.
The coward creatures are the prey of man;
And he who fears like them belies his form.
But we are open to intrusion here;
800    Into this chamber – Nay, but you shall come.

              *Exeunt into an apartment that opens in the centre*
*of the scene.*
              *Enter* YAMOS.

YAMOS: I will not credit what Orooko thinks:
His mind has ever been adverse to all
Antonio's mighty purposes. Old age,
That make experience wisdom, grows to folly,
And the good man may have outliv'd discretion. –
It is not, cannot be, that one so great,
So lofty and prospective in his virtue,
Should fall to such perdition. But my Idda!
O Heaven and Nature! if 'tis not disease
810    That hath the sweet love of her bosom chang'd –
Ah, who art thou, so ghastly and so grim,
With grasped dagger, and blanch'd quiv'ring lip,
That beckons me towards horror? – Revenge!
Hence from my soul, delirious suggestion.
Murder Antonio! What hideous guilt
Must in the issue of such treach'ry lie,
That my unhappy spirit should devise
Indemnity so terrible? – No, no:
They are not guilty, and my mind is cleft
820    From all propriety in thinking them.
O righteous Heaven! with some oblivious blessing,
Quench in my memory Orooko's venom,
And heal my heart to confidence again. –

              *He goes to the door by which* ANTONIO *and* IDDA
*had retired, and on opening it starts back:* ANTONIO *and* IDDA *come*

*from within and fly off at one side, while* OROOKO *and attendants en-*
*ter from the other: after a pause* YAMOS *comes forward in a state of*
*stupefaction.*

OROOKO: O hapless Yamos, what unhallow'd vision
Enchants thine eyes to look that way so wild? –
Speak to me, Yamos, tell me what thou see'st? –

YAMOS: Nothing – they are not there – they were not there –
I saw them not – I thought but what did seem –
(*to Orooko.*) Art thou not, wretch, some false bewildering devil,
830    Mocking my sight with good Orooko's form?
O thou hast bred with thy soul-tainting breath
Thoughts of such horrible and hungry crave,
That I must needs be wicked – It is true!
A sword, a sword! – Now well I know the cause
Why he enticed us to unbelt our swords:
He fear'd that in detection we might use them,
And so made passage for a safe escape.

OROOKO: Speak you, sir, of the stranger?

YAMOS: Of the fiend!
840    He came to me so piteous and forlorn,
That my weak heart could not but do him kindness.
He seem'd to me so wond'rous and so wise,
That my poor thoughts could not but do him homage.
O little thought I when religiously
He used to tell me of the luring wiles
With which the foe of God seduces man,
That he was him, and then betraying me.

OROOKO: Still you are free, though Idda be his victim.

YAMOS: O Idda, Idda! Rose of my delight!
850    The odious worm voluptuous with thy beauty,
Has turn'd my love to loathing – Damn her, damn her!

OROOKO: Does other proof than my suspicion move you?

YAMOS: O yes.

OROOKO: What! – who?

YAMOS: My eyes!

OROOKO: How, Yamos! where!

YAMOS: Earth, make me part of thy insensate mass;
Let me be kneaded by the heel to clay.

*throws himself down.*

Rather than bear the memory of that vision!

860    OROOKO: O thou renewing spirit of the air,
Whose genial power informs the sleeping spring
When to put forth her young hands to the ray,
Revive to hope the withering soul of Yamos.

# ACT IV, SCENE ONE

*An Apartment.*
ANTONIO (*solo.*)

The sin was **Nature's** when she made me thus: –
These limbs she moulded; link'd the vital chain
Of lively pulses circling through my heart;
Gave that love-darting lustre to my eyes
Which the fond fair so willingly obey;
And tun'd my voice to that persuasive mood,
870  Which wins so easily whate'er I ask: –
Can I then doubt the promptings of desire,
Come not as issue and effect from Nature,
And if they do so, wherein lies the ill?
I cannot choose, when beauty meets my sight,
But instantly to feel its thrilling charm
Enticing to embrace. Good is but pleasure,
And that which pleases must be good to me;
If others find it harm, is the fault mine?

*Enter* ARAK.

Arak, my friend, approach – Why stand you back?
880  Why look you on me with such awful dread?
What would you with me? Why these alter'd looks?

ARAK: The consecrated elders of our tribes,
Convened by old Orooko, send for you.
I am their messenger; say, will you come?

ANTONIO: But tell me first, why thus you are so sad –
My sin is but an error of my blood,
Call'd into action by the queen's alluring.

ARAK: The consecrated elders of our tribes,
Convened by old Orooko, send for you.
90   I am their messenger; say, will you come?

ANTONIO: Well, I will go: but Arak, do inform me –

*Exit* ARAK.

My friend! he, gone! without a word, retir'd! –
Save but his solemn summons twice repeated.
O vain delusion! to persuade myself
That the delinquency of mine offence
Belong'd to Nature, or that others would
Ascribe my guilt to the primeval sin.
It is not what a man thinks of himself
That constitutes him bad or virtuous,
00   But as his actions touch the hearts of others. –
Yes, that same bounteous and divine endowment
Which fills the bosom with alert aversion
Against all odious and injurious things,
Excites the hate that guilty deeds inspire. –
The loathsome scorpion, whose envenom'd fang
Strikes cruel death, nor the remorseless vulture,
That plucks the eyeball of the hero dead;
O not the yellow and abhorred worm,
That riots on the breast where youthful love,
10   Once hop'd for bliss, is to the sense so hateful,
As I am now to the affrighten'd thoughts
Of this confiding, good, and gentle race.

*Exit.*

# ACT IV, SCENE TWO

*A Vestibule.*
YAMOS *and* OROOKO.

OROOKO: It cannot be that this deceitful man
Derives his blood from our primeval sire:
He nor his nation, not the God he worships,
Can have affinity with us or ours.
We, till his fatal tread deform'd our shore,
Did ever deem that chief most worthy honor,
Who least appear'd to need another's aid.
He would have taught you but for this blest crime,
I call it blest, since it dissolves the spell
Of his deceit – yes, had persuaded you
That they deserve the ritual of the knee,
Who are themselves of all mankind most helpless.
Before the round of many moons had wan'd,
We should have seen the ties reciprocal,
Of chief and follower slacken'd from all use,
And man to man in opposition set
Upon the plea of rank inherited.
Has he not told that in the eastern world,
The man most honor'd is the slave that tends
The largest count of slaves? Were not his arts
To quench the instinct which the mighty spirit
Bestow'd to guide us, giving the conceits
Of human frailty and invented reason
Hostile supremacy o'er nature's wisdom? –
Were such the customs, such the precepts ever
Of your great sires who never own'd a slave,
But conscious lords of all the breathing world,
Held each with each th' equality of kings.

Their only vassals were the prey that paid
A prompt obedience to the speedy shafts
Which levied their revenue – You attend not?

YAMOS: Be you, Orooko, judge, I am not fit:
The vengeful influence of his treachery
Distorts to me the rightful aim of justice.

OROOKO: No, Yamos, no; this solemn cause demands
That you should prove to the audacious stranger
Our old inborn superiority.

950    It must not seem that our selected chief
Should e'er in his great office stand perplex'd –
What! shall we hold the frail and feeble wretch
Who shrinks at the afflictions of a wound,
Rejected of our tribes, and not require
From you, our chief, that firm impartial mind
Which would adjudicate against itself?

YAMOS: Against itself! – You know me well, Orooko,
Nor have I swerv'd from my integrity;
But I do feel my spirit apt with ire,

960    To be vindictive by the sword of justice.

OROOKO: How! is thy nature then indeed so tainted,
That all its hate of the exotic crime
Is turn'd on him who had thy own permission?

YAMOS: Much I can bear, Orooko, from thy chiding,
But chafe me not too far – my rage is hungry,
And will have prey before it is appeas'd.

OROOKO: Do you refuse the duty we expect?

YAMOS: How now, old man, you frown rebelliously?

OROOKO: What if I, in the name of all the tribes,

970    Assert the privilege the elders ever
Have held in times of public jeopardy?

YAMOS: And what was that?

OROOKO: To change the ruling chief.

YAMOS: What have I done to cause me such dishonor?

OROOKO: You do refuse to execute your trust.

YAMOS: I would refuse it in this, my own cause,
But I do not refuse.

OROOKO: Then follow me
To where the assembled elders of the tribes
980      Have form'd the circle of avenging justice,
And wait but for your coming – This way, sir.

*Exeunt.*

# ACT IV, SCENE THREE

*An Apartment.*
IDDA.

O what is this that weighs upon my heart
Like the oppression of a dead man's hand –
Methinks all nature is alarm'd around,
Rous'd by the omens of some dreadful change,
Whose coming horror far and black descried
No mortal can describe. I seem to stand
Like one deserted on the frozen sea,
While o'er the waves, beyond the stretching ice,
990 Dark as mid night, a brooding tempest glooms –
O'er head, the sea-birds screaming seek the land –
The bold seal-hunters hurrying without prey,
Look wildly wond'ring at the fated wretch,
And sullenly speed home – Loud under foot,
Th' imprison'd ocean raging to be free,
Tears with the earthquake's strength. – What is my doom?

*Enter* MORA.

What will they do with me – what is decreed?

MORA: There is a rock, two bow-shots from the shore,
Whose tangled head, till half the tide is run,
000 Lies hid beneath the waves.

IDDA: Well, Mora, well.

MORA: What time to-night the evening star shall rise
Above the mountains, that mysterious rock
Will from his forehead lift the watry veil.

IDDA: O Mora, be not so oracular,
But tell me quickly all. What horror waits
On the appearing of that dismal sign?

MORA: I can but only echo what I heard.

IDDA: Proceed, proceed, there's boding in thy voice;
1010      And the sad portent of these solemn eyes,
Alarms me more than were the sun eclips'd,
And the bright stars that gem the winter's night,
Seen through the myst'ry of the summer's noon. –
When the black forehead of the rock appears,
What hideous work begins?

MORA: In silence then,
Two sable boats shall slowly quit the shore –

IDDA: Bearing me and Antonio? No? What then?

MORA: In one shall sit the dumb dejected man,
1020      Who knows all things that other mortals know,
But wants the organs to embody speech –
And he shall bear in his right hand –

IDDA: O heavens!

MORA: A funeral torch, to kindle on the rock
The signal fire of death.

IDDA: The other boat?

MORA: Shall follow freighted with a sentenc'd victim.

IDDA: Which?

MORA: You.

1030      IDDA: Alone?

# THE APOSTATE

MORA: Alone.

IDDA: Tell me what then?

MORA: The boats will leave you on the rock to perish,
With no companion but the deadman's fire,
By which, when the refluent tide has quench'd it,
Th' assembled tribes, collected on the shore,
May know your life was with the flame extinguish'd.

IDDA: My throat is parching and my breath becomes
Like suffocating ashes – air! air! air!

*Exeunt.*

# ACT IV, SCENE FOUR

*A Wood: the town seen beyond. The Elders of the tribes assembled in a
semi-circle on the ground.*

OROOKO, YAMOS, ANTONIO, &c.

1040     OROOKO: This warmth is counterfeit, notions so fanciful,
Spring not in Nature from th' impassion'd heart –
They are but fire-flies, startled from their resting,
And not the inborn blossoms of the bough –
Answer expressly to the charge we make?

ANTONIO: How may I to your stern demand reply?
I own the guilt! I ask the punishment!
If aught the tortures of your fiercest fires
Can add of anguish to the thoughts I suffer.
But Oh, forbear to blame the truth I taught,
1050     Nor think the sin of my ill-destin'd frame
Can taint the bright intelligence of Heaven,
To which I am but as some hateful reptile,
Whose slimy back reflects the glorious sun.
O royal Yamos, noblest injured man,
I seek no mercy for my odious self,
Though thy blest nature, form'd for higher good
Than the heroic spirit e'er inspir'd,
Would e'en to me, whose devil-serving passions
Have made such wreck of all thy soul held dearest,
1060     Find naught so easy as to grant me pardon.
Let not the thought, that my detested crime
Is ever sequence to the taste of truth,
Enter the temple of thy blameless heart;

But onward bravely in thy great career,
And be to all succeeding ages known,
As he who first amidst the Atlantine wilds,
The altars of eternal knowledge raised.

YAMOS: But what will that avail?

ANTONIO: (*aside*) Ha! does he doubt?

070     YAMOS: Turn not away, I speak not to reproach –
Unhappy man, I ask thee but to tell
How will the praises of the far-unborn
Repay the sacrifice that must be made,
Before the fruitage ripen into use?
O yes, Antonio, once I thought like thee,
That to be class'd with those immortal kings,
Whom all the sages of thy eastern world
Deem wisdom best devoted in revering,
Were a triumphant recompense for braving
080     My fathers' ghosts, whose unembodied voices
Spoke sternly to my thoughts. Alas, when oft
Amidst the falling trees we fell'd to raise
Yon guilty roofs, I heard them sigh around,
My fearful heart had foretaste of its woe,
And felt, it knew not why, th' alarm of guilt;
But still the flatt'ring pageant of renown
Rose bright in view, and my enchanted mind
Beheld as 'twere an image of myself,
High rais'd refulgent, while in spreading circles
090     Appear'd the millions of succeeding times,
Filling the vast horizon to its bound,
And shouting loud my name. The dream is past!
And yet methinks I am not well awake.
The hideous nightmare sits upon my breast,
And while I see around these towers and domes,
I strangely hope my sense is but abus'd
By some delusion of unwholesome sleep.

Idda, my love! art thou not at my side?
Where art thou, Idda? – O where is my love!

1100    OROOKO: Yamos, Yamos, what madness fires thy mind,
That thus in the great synod of the Elders
Thou darest this breach of all solemnity?

YAMOS: See'st thou that pallid wretch, whose evil eyes
Have glanc'd eternal blight on all my hopes?

OROOKO: Come to thy seat again, and give the sentence.

YAMOS: But will the word of power, that dooms to death,
Restore my bosom to its wonted calm?

OROOKO: This wildness must not further be endured. –
Never before did warrior of our tribe
1110    Insult the presence of th' assembled Elders,
With such a rapture of entranced passion.

YAMOS: Never before were any of our tribe
Pain'd with the anguish of a grief like mine.

OROOKO: (*to the Elders*) Ye, who have felt in youth's
         imperious prime,
The goading insult of a foeman's frown,
Rouse your bold spirits into leaping rage,
That would not be restrain'd; blame not in him
These transports at irreparable wrong,
But pardon his irreverence – take your place –
1120    Come, noble Yamos, look, the Elders wait.

YAMOS: What would they more? – Antonio has confess'd,
And Idda ye have doom'd – O why should I
Be further tortured in this dire probation?

OROOKO: Say but the sentence, and it will be finish'd.

YAMOS: Then let him live.

52

OROOKO: How live?

YAMOS: Aye, and may Heaven
Punish his crimes with constancy of health,
Prolong'd beyond the utmost term that love,
130    E'er in the hour of rapture wish'd to live.
For he is noble, and the sense of guilt,
With keener agony than tonguing flames
Lick to the bone, will be his punishment.

OROOKO: Shall he live also free?

YAMOS: Yes, free and public. –
Beware that none of the accustom'd homage
Towards him be withheld – else might the thought,
The angry thought that springs from punishment,
Defeat th' intended horror of our sentence. –
140    Antonio, friend! why dost thou hang thy head,
And clasp thy hands distracted in the air?
Once thou didst tell me of some secret law,
By which the evil germ in different breasts,
Holds mystic sympathy, and to ill deeds
E'en passing strangers suddenly constrains –
This truth of all you taught, I find first true,
The devilish charm of your perfidious guilt
Stirs in the latent vices of my blood,
And makes me cunning that I may be cruel.

*Exeunt.*

# ACT V, SCENE ONE

*A Street open to the sea, the rock seen.*
ANTONIO.

Shull I thuo oolitary ever live,
And in these haunts, scenes of my pride and triumph,
Alone like one of those dejected ghosts,
Whom poets in their mournful frenzies deem
The hov'ring witnesses of joyous rites,
Held by the friends they thought would weep their death,
Move unregarded, or be seen with fear? –
It were a state less hideous to be doom'd
To constant penance in some dread cadav'ry,
Where the dim death-light shows the mould'ring dead,
Grinning as 'twere in horrible derision,
As the contemptuous spirit of decay
Throws from its scite the long unfasten'd scull.[1] –
To sit alone in some forgotten ruin,
Far in some distant long untravell'd waste,
Where, save the thirsty serpent's ceaseless hiss,
No sound is ever heard: – To see from thence
The red and arid sun'd unvaried orb,
Roll o'er the brazen skies and sink to night,
Day after day, in dull monotony,
And all the story of remembrance lost,
But one black thought, the memory of the crime,
Would not, methinks, be such a solitude,
As that which now environs me around,
In the denying looks of former friends. –

---

[1]A scite is the location of a capital property. A scull is a small oar used by a single rower.

Here comes my enemy – O thought unjust;
He was no foe, had I myself been true.

*Enter* OROOKO.

OROOKO: There stands the wretch so woeful and forlorn,
That my relenting nature melts to see him.

30     ANTONIO: I would speak to him, and enquire the doom
Pronounced upon the queen. He will not answer,
And yet there's more compassion in his eyes
Than e'er I witness'd, more than they express'd
When hapless Yamos sav'd me from the sea.

*The sound of a shell or horn is heard.*

OROOKO: Hark! the sad sounding of the funeral shell,
Gives dismal warning that the hour approaches.

ANTONIO: Tell me, Orooko, what these sounds denote?

OROOKO: The prelude of a solemn sacrifice. –
Thou start'st! –

40     ANTONIO: A sacrifice!

OROOKO: Yes, to our Gods!
The Gods of nature and of innocence!

ANTONIO: Ah, stern old man, dost thou impute to mine,
The instigations that have made me guilty;
Or think'st thou that my better part denies
The justice of the punishment I suffer. –
Now, that no more my faith may taint thy tribes,
Nor thin the worshippers around thy altars,
Wilt thou, for once, allow me to repeat
50     The grounds of my religion.

OROOKO: Fatal man!
Dost thou presume with me to try thine arts? –
Spirit of everlasting life and light,
Avert their influence, and keep me firm,
Against this new contrition that begins
To mine into my heart!
(*to* ANTONIO)
What would'st thou say,
Would'st thou rehearse to me that tale of fancy,
Which thou hast told of worlds beyond the stars,
Where vital brightness in the beams of wisdom,
Still kindles with intelligence eterne;
And bid me break the bread and drink the wine,
As my acceptance of admission there?
Or would'st thou frighten me, if I refuse,
By the grim terrors of that other religion,
That dread abyss beneath the midway ocean, –
Beneath the deep foundations of the isles, –
That hollow vast of everlasting fires –
Sapping the arch on which great Nature stands,
Predoom'd to fall with hideous crash, and hurl
Into the billowy and exasperate flames,
There sink for ever and for ever down, –
Would'st thou tell this, and ask me to believe?

ANTONIO: No, Sir, and yet by your impassion'd voice,
You seem to tremble, lest it may be true. –
But I would tell you how th' eternal mind
Abhors the guilt of its corporeal agent,
And ask you whence such strange division springs,
If that which thanks, and that which acts in man,
May not exist apart?

OROOKO: And if they may?

ANTONIO: Shall then the thoughtful element be left
In unappropriated listlessness,

When into dust its mortal dwelling falls?
Or should we deem all the recoil of action
Fix'd to the limit of our biding here;
And lift the aims of human thought no higher
Than the mean instincts of our sensual wishes? –
90     If man be as you say but animal,
Why am I punish'd, where was Idda's crime?

*Sounds of the shell.*

These dismal sounds of sacrifice again!
And this way rolls the throng!

OROOKO: O stay not here,
Stay not to witness what must here be done.
Alas, Antonio, thy mysterious thoughts
Perplex my spirit in an awful hour.

*Exeunt.*
*Enter* SEBI *and* MORA.

MORA: Where shall I fly that I may but forget
The hideous look of horror and despair,
100     With which she glared on me her last farewell.
O father, father, hold my bursting head,
Her glance was lightning, and has fired my brain.

SEBI: Unhappy child!

MORA: Do you not hear her cries?
Hark!

SEBI: All is silent.

*the shells sound.*

MORA: Ha! the shells again,
She struggles still, they drag her to the shore.
O bear me hence, support me, father, hence –
I dare not that way look, and yet my eyes,
Charm'd by her horror, will not be withdrawn.

SEBI: Why will you linger, asking still to fly,
Come, dearest Mora, come?

MORA: They hold her fast,
The dumb torchbearer steps into the boat;
They bind the victim – wretches, hold! hold! hold!

*Exeunt towards the side by which they entered.*

# ACT V, SCENE TWO

*An Apartment.*
YAMOS *and* ARAK, *and* Attendants.

YAMOS: Heard ye that shriek? It came upon my ear
As the quick lightning flashes on the eye,
Startling the soul – How awful is this silence
Which has succeeded to that glance of sound!
Methinks it has affinity with death,
And should be named with epithets of blackness.
Where is Orooko?

ARAK: At the sacrifice.

YAMOS: What sacrifice! Why dost thou turn away –
It was the victim's cry then that I heard? –
O 'twas my Idda, loveliest, still belov'd! –
But I forget that justice claim'd her doom,
And Guilt with clammy and opprobrious clutch,
More hideous than the mouldering grasp of death,
Tore our incorporate hearts asunder.

*the shells sound.*

Hark! again, O Idda! down my heart, lie down.
Summon the choristers, bid them sing shrill, –
Wake all your instruments of wildest sound,
And drown th' afflicting discord of her cries.

*Music.*

No more, no more – Tell me, is it yet done?
Has the bright star, that should to night arise
At the returning of the tide, appear'd?

ARAK: It just begins to glimmer o'er the sea.

YAMOS: O ere the tide shall reach its wonted bourn,
The beauteous orb, that crown'd my life's fair dawn,
Must set for ever in the gloomy wave. –
Has not Orooko come?

ARAK: We have not sent.

YAMOS: Why am I not obey'd, wherefore is this,
That you deny the duty of your place?
Go bring him instantly – yet stop – not yet. –
She may not yet have reach'd the fatal rock.
How long time thinkest thou? –

ARAK: What would you, sir?

YAMOS: No matter, Arak – we'll towards the shore, –
Command Antonio to attend me there.

*Exeunt.*

# ACT V, SCENE THREE

*The Rock and fire – The coast and town seen in perspective, the boats pass.*

### IDDA.

O they are gone, and will return no more,
And I am left to perish here alone!
Stay yet awhile – stay but to see me die!
Suspend your oars till the returning wave
Has quench'd my life and this dull flame together.
Alas! alas! they heed not my entreaty!
But swift and steadily make to the shore! –
The shore is throng'd, piled with a countless crowd;
Hear me, O hear me! – O my feeble voice
Fails in the midway of the dismal distance,
And I am here an off'ring on death's altar,
Like some lost wretch by eager heirs interr'd,
Awak'ning from his trance within the grave –
O horror, horror, is there then no hope!

*Exit.*

# ACT V, SCENE FOUR

*A Street.*
OROOKO, SEBI *and* ANTONIO.

OROOKO: What would the crowd with all these pitched
   brands?

SEBIS: They think that when the waves o'erwhelm the queen,
Yamos will then restore our ancient rites,
And bid the town be fir'd.

OROOKO: Who told them that?

SEBI: 'Tis but their fancy.

OROOKO: And yet they prepare,
As if th' ordonnance of it were proclaim'd!
Such strong assurance in the public mind,
Denotes some feeling in the frame of things,
That proves the pregnant future almost ripe
With some great offspring in the line of fate.
'Tis as the sadness that pervades the air,
Before the coming thunder. In the town
Far-stretching necks from the close-crowded windows,
And all eyes turned the same way in the streets,
Do not more certainly presage th' approach
Of solemn pageants, than parentless rumors,
Foretell th' occurrence of some high event.

SEBI: You seem alarm'd – I thought you would rejoice.

OROOKO: Hast thou heard this, Antonio?

SEBI: He's entranc'd,
And hears not what is said.

OROOKO: Antonio?

ANTONIO: Well!

OROOKO: See'st thou the throng so busily intent –
Look how the young men cleave the splint'ring pine,
While in the seething pitch their fathers dip,
The riven fragments which the children gather,
And serious women in their aprons bring.
What think'st thou of this solemn preparation?

ANTONIO: O righteous Heaven! now is my doom complete,
Must that blest germ which I had planted here,
For my aggression be so soon destroy'd.

OROOKO: Who told thee that?

ANTONIO: You to the truths I taught,
Ascribe the guilty working of my blood,
And to suppress the truth will burn the town.

OROOKO: Antonio!

ANTONIO: Speak, what mean you!

OROOKO: I believe,
If that which thinks in us survives the tomb,
That thou wast right in teaching us to rise
Still more and more out of the sensual life,
Into th' intelligence which after death
May raise our being to a higher state.

ANTONIO kneels.

SEBI: What sudden blessing dissipates his gloom,
And makes him thus in thankful transports kneel.

# THE APOSTATE

*Enter ARAK.*

ARAK: Unhappy Yamos, wand'ring in his mind,
And with the crowd wild-mingling on the shore,
Commands you to attend.

OROOKO: Antonio rise.
Alas, I would thou might'st remain behind.
For at the sight of thee his rage again
May burst in outrage fatal to the wish.
Which my expanding heart begins to cherish.

ANTONIO: Come let us go. Whatever may befall
Cannot be evil, if on you descends
Th' inspiring mantle of immortal truth.
Yes! o'er the funeral ashes of the town,
A pure celestial light shall ever shine,
To which the scatter'd tribes will oft return,
In holy pilgrimage, if you will guide
Their wand'ring spirits in the devious way
Of knowledge, which, alas, so slipp'ry winds
Through tangling brakes, where many a serpent lurks.

*Exeunt.*

# ACT V, SCENE FIVE

*The Shore – The rock seen at a distance, nearly covered, the star high in the Heavens, and the water rising. – The crowd of the town on all sides. – YAMOS with his back towards the rock.*

*Enter OROOKO, ANTONIO, ARAK and SEBI.*

YAMOS: Approach, Antonio, come – thou wast my friend,
I did believe thou wast, for I was thine,
And lov'd thee well, yes, I was kind to thee,
And lov'd thee for the kindness I bestow'd,
More than the misers of thy distant world
Doat on the coffers where they lay their treasures.
How hast thou answer'd my confiding friendship?
But come, draw near, why dost thou shrink apart?
The ill which thou hast done will soon be ended.
10 Behold this throng, whose every eye is turned
Towards a part of the dark rising sea,
Where I can never look – What see'st thou there?
Well may'st thou tremble – Tell me what thou see'st.

ANTONIO: A dim red flame.

YAMOS: And nothing more? – no sign?

ANTONIO: Yes, ever and anon it is eclipsed,
As if some busy figure intervened.

YAMOS: Idda is there alone – Nay, do not sink:
Thou hast a part in this terrific rite,
20 And I expect the full and dread performance –
Attend and answer me – What now appears?

ANTONIO: O take my life, and save me from this torment.

YAMOS: Be mute in all, but to my questioning –
Burns yet the light?

ANTONIO: It does.

YAMOS: See'st thou no sign?

ANTONIO: The billows rolling on the rising tide,
By fits obscure its dim and lurid glare.

YAMOS: Does it still burn? – Slave, slave, perform thy task.
What means that deep and universal sigh?

ANTONIO: The light is quench'd. –

YAMOS: My Idda is no more!
And the suppress'd affliction of my soul
May now take all its frenzy.

OROOKO: Hold his hand!

*ANTONIO stabs himself and falls.*

YAMOS: Ha! which of you did this?

OROOKO: Himself.

YAMOS: Himself!

OROOKO: With his own guilty hand he aim'd the knife.

YAMOS: Stop! touch him not! lest the self-murder'd corpse
Cause some contagion worse than this new crime.
Now, now, Orooko, loud, with all thy voice,
Command the sacrifice.

OROOKO: What sacrifice?

YAMOS: A victim meet for our apostacy;
Lead on the multitude and fire the town!

OROOKO: Stay, Yamos, stay; suspend thy rash design;
For if crime of this self-slain arose
From causes adverse to his truth and science,
50   What deeper guilt had stain'd his short career,
But for their blest restraining – Heavenly truth,
Like the bright sun's unquenchable effulgence,
Which, from the foul and aguey fen, exhales
The foggy pestilence and dries its poison;
Receives no blemish from terrestrial vapor;
Serene, sublime, it holds its destin'd course
Above the momentary clouds that shadow
The human Chrysalis, whose mortal term,
By the slight tissue, spun from its own breast
60   Is pass'd in darkness and captivity.

YAMOS: (to OROOKO) Ha! is the demon that in him deluded
Transferr'd to thee, who wast of all the world
The most oppos'd to his great mysteries? –
Then spread thy wings, and speed into the sun-shine!

*He stabs OROOKO who falls.*

Come now, Atlantines, hurl your brands around,
Till but the ashes of the sacrifice
Be all the trace of our apostacy. –
Ghosts of our sires, pause in your airy chase,
And, as the flames of these proud towers ascend,
70   Around in hov'ring circles, view them burn.

*Curtain falls as the town is set on fire.*

**THE END.**

# REMARKS ON THE APOSTATE

### Remarks on *The Apostate*[1]

The story on which this drama is founded, was probably suggested by that obscure rumor which had prevailed from the days of
Plato, to those of Columbus, respecting the existence of the western
continent. It is, however, a subject, perhaps, more suitable to descrip-
tive narration, than calculated to produce such a degree of dramatic
effect as would render it impressive in representation.

The motives of the author in making choice of a fable so entirely
fictitious, seem to have been of a two-fold nature; the originality of
the incidents which it allowed him to introduce, and the opportunity
which it afforded to him of placing the two great crimes, peculiar
to the civilized state, Adultery and Suicide, in a strong and striking
light.

Several of the ocular circumstances, though questionable as his
inventions, will readily be admitted to equal in the terrific any thing
which the stage exhibits. The situation of Idda left to perish on the
rock, is one of this description, but it is perhaps not thoroughly dramatic; for when she compares herself to a person untimely interred
reviving within the grave, she only gives us another view of her own
horror without adding any new feature to the frightfulness of the
original idea, or eliciting any thought which might enable us to par-
ticipate in her feelings.

The expiring of the penal fire seen by the spectators, is founded
on a real occurrence mentioned in the life of Admiral Byron; and the
imagination cannot conceive any spectacle more awfully interesting.
Had it been an invention, the author might have obtained the praise

---

[1] These "remarks" appear following the play in *The New British Theatre* (1814),
Pp. 346-348 (page number 348 is incorrectly numbered "483." These remarks are
most likely written by Henry Colburn (1784-1855). See Introduction (Footnote 1).

of contriving one of the most sublime scenic spectacles in the whole range of the drama.

The characters, like the incidents, are perhaps rather possible existences than delineations of human beings. In Orooko, however, there are traits of individuality, which make it probable that it was in some degree intended for a portrait. Antonio, as a development of constitutional licentiousness counteracting moral intentions, may lay claim to some consideration. He is of a species familiar enough to the stage, but of a class that authors have been diffident in embodying so fully. Yamos is only a young Othello, and Arak is not sufficiently prominent to interest us much in his fate. The character of Idda, is not graced with any amiable feeling. It may be doubted if the author has acted judiciously in making so naked a delineation of the debasing effects of the animal propensity; for the fastidious spirit of modern criticism is offended if the snaky length of Sin be not concealed by a petticoat.

The train of moral sentiment in this piece is evidently derived from Rousseau's celebrated essay against the arts and sciences;[2] and the reader of voyages and travels will probably discover an indirect endeavour of the author to give a fabulous account of the origin of that inexplicable antipathy which the Indians of America cherish towards the effects of civilization. He informs us that the ideas which he has given to Orooko, were principally drawn from an authentic description which he had received of the manners and notions of the Indians, from a person who once spent a hunting season with a party that was in the practice of making an annual visit to the city of Philadelphia. In this respect, the piece possesses a degree of originality, *wholly* independent of the poet, and of a kind which deserves attention without reference either to the verse or the language.

The reader alone can determine whether the subject of this play has been so managed as to interest the mind; for whatever may be the claims of originality, as to invention or appropriation of incidents, the tragedy can have but little merit as a drama, if the story is not interestingly developed.

---

[2] *A Discourse on the Moral Effects of the Arts and Sciences* (1750), by Jean-Jacques Rousseau.

We are requested to state, that the outline of Antonio's character was suggested by the manner in which Mr. Kean[3] performs the character of Iago – It certainly has appeared to many good dramatic judges, that the air of libertine gaiety which that excellent actor assumes in this part, does not accord with the general impression which the text of Shakespeare makes in perusal. Perhaps the objection made to Mr. Kean's performance is well founded. The versatility of his talents requires a various part to produce their full effect, and the Iago is so uniformly a villain, that the defect of Mr. Kean may be owing to an attempt to vary the odious sameness of the character.

Iago is one of the strongest drawn, but the worst completed of all Shakespeare's characters. It is equally unnaturally wicked and consistent. The attempt of Mr. Kean to make it more human, is a proof of his good taste; and his failure in this part is rather an honor to his judgment, than a disgrace to his powers.

---

[3]Edmund Kean (1787-1833), a celebrated Shakespearean stage actor.

# THE NEW ATLANTIS – AN AMERICAN LEGEND

## John Galt
### (1831)

*Introduction by John Galt*

Beyond the Allegany mountains,[1] and even in the regions of Canada to the north-west of the St. Lawrence, are many traces of an extinct race. Enormous earthen constructions of walls and ramparts, inclosing extensive spaces, more like the sites of cities than of fortresses or entrenched camps, are still visible. Not many miles to the north of Little York, [2] the capital of Upper Canada, one of those aboriginal works may be seen, in such preservation that its form may be easily traced. Circleville, one of the most considerable towns in the State of Ohio, is built within a primeval enclosure of the same kind; and in the wild countries comprehended southward within the courses of the Missouri and the Mississippi, still more interesting remains are met with – such as extensive cemeteries and places of particular sepulture – all indicating that, in some distant epoch of antiquity, a numerous population *did* inhabit there.

It is, however, remarkable, that in the midst of so many monuments of comparative civilization – comparative with that of the Indians – no works of art have been discovered, except stone weapons, and, in one or two places, funeral urns, resembling, though in a rude degree, the Etruscan vases; and even these are supposed to be of more recent origin. The inference from this fact is, that the works alluded to were either the hasty fabrics of invaders, or the temporary erections of a rude people under the tuition of some extraordinary mind.

---

[1]See my Introduction (pages)
[2]Toronto

The Indians have no traditions on the subject; but if consulted concerning them, they speak vaguely, as if they were the relics of a people that had passed away. They have, however, among themselves, curious notions that the simplicity of the savage life was dictated to them by the experience of ancient wisdom; and the following Legendary Tale is an attempt to assign something like a poetical cause, founded on the circumstances of the country, for that remarkable opinion.

### The New Atlantis – An American Legend
### John Galt
### (1831)

Before the discovery of America, a numerous people inhabited the savannahs and table land between the Mississippi, the Missouri, and the Pacific Ocean. They were a simple race, and lived by the arrow and the spear. They worshipped the Great Spirit of Nature in his manifestations, and in all things acted with heedless innocence and frankness of heart.

A tremendous hurricane, accompanied by earthquakes and the overflowing of subterranean waters, visited the country: for many days, the winds raged as if the bridle had been thrown on the neck of the tempest; the lightnings did not flash only, but burned, as it were, with shooting flames. It was a time as if chaos had come again; and the terrified inhabitants of those spacious prairies and green savannahs fled in despair from the rising waters of the great lakes, which overflowed their banks, and seamed the country with many new streams.

At last, the struggles and spasms of the earth and the air subsided, the torrents contracted their bounds and their devastations, calm was restored, the sun looked out upon the reviving world, and the waves of the lakes, the lagoons, and the ocean, unfurled their hoary manes to the morning.

Oroon,[3] the son of a venerated chieftain who had perished, on the return of tranquility happened, with a vast multitude of his people, to

---

[3] named Orooko in the earlier play

be seated on a promontory, mournfully contemplating the desolation around, and irresolute of returning to their former homes. While they were ruminating there, some of the Indians, for such we must call them, who had been in quest of fish along the shore, returned in great agitation, and described an enormous creature which they had seen stranded, with many wings, and horns as tall as trees.

Oroon, attended by the multitude, went to see this stupendous thing; and, in approaching towards it, a creature, much in form like themselves, came to meet them, and, with many reverences, by his gestures implored their protection. Oroon received him with the kindness of his own innocent magnanimity, and according to the benevolent maxims which the Great Spirit dictates to his worshippers.

The name of this mysterious stranger was Atlanthus, as he afterwards taught the Indians to call him when he had learned their language; and the mighty thing which they had imagined to be a creature of the ocean, he informed them, was a ship, which had brought him and many others in quest of their world.

Atlanthus was, according to the legend, a man possessed of more wisdom and knowledge than all the Indians. He not only expounded many things which their sagacity could not comprehend, but, with simple signs, he made a memory by which those whom he taught to know the secret, could recall the very language of the dead. Oroon regarded him with worship, and the Indians venerated him as something greater and better than man.

When he understood the Indian language, he taught Oroon knowledge, and science, and art; he instructed him to divide his people into classes, to build cities, to separate those who laboured in the towns from those who tilled the earth; he revealed to them the existence of a visible manifestation of the Great Spirit; and taught them all those things which were esteemed great and glorious in the regions from which he had come.

Among the people of Oroon, there was an old chief of the name of Icab, who, when he saw the cities rising, and the licentious changes that were taking place in the old and primitive customs of his countrymen, reviled the innovations of Atlanthus; and, gathering together many of the elders of the tribes with their families, he retired far into the inland country, to avoid the contagion of the new rites.

It had happened, a short time before the terrible devastation, that Oroon had chosen for his bride Arutha, the most beautiful daughter of the Indians: he loved her with his entire heart, and her affection for him was equally measureless. They were two in person, but one in spirit; and the beauty of their attachment was the admiration of all the people.

When some time had elapsed, and the great city of Atlantis, which Atlanthus had planned, was lifting its magnificent forehead above the woods, Oroon observed, with dismay, that Arutha was often dissatisfied with his kindness. She avoided him, she answered peevishly to his kindest enquiries, and shunned him when she could. At the same time, Atlanthus also was greatly changed. He retired from Oroon, and was often seen with melancholy looks, and as a man afflicted with some unspeakable anguish. The most skilful of the Indians were called to administer to the strange malady of Arutha, but all their herbs and simples produced no effect; and Atlanthus' dejection seemed to be also incurable.

Oroon, greatly grieved at the decay of Arutha's affection, and deploring the equally inveterate distemper of Atlanthus, sent Arak, a messenger, to Icab, who was skilful in diseases, to beseech him to come and assist the invalids.

Arak went alone into the forest, and, after many days' travelling, he came to an open space beside a great lake, into which a vast river was tumbling over many cataracts. It was a scene full of the old solemnities of nature, and he stood contemplating it with that awe and dread which the spirit of solitude inspires. As he was looking on that calm magnificence, the old man, Icab, came towards him, and, with a severe voice, enquiring why he had presumed to enter those unprofaned solitudes.

"Arak," he cried; "thou hast forsaken thy father's gods; and I can never more lift my hands above thee to implore, as I was wont, their blessings on thy young head. Oh, ye unknown, dreadful, and beneficent Powers, whom all artless creatures worship, pardon these tears, and forgive my weak heart, that would forget the sin of this young man, and which yearns to receive him still, as your Gracious Spirit has taught me to feel for all human kind. Alas! it is true that I could not think such things possible, as that man would presume to select his God."

Icab then fell upon the neck of Arak and wept.

"I bring you," said Arak, "a message from the king."

"What would he now with me?" exclaimed Icab: "he might spare the little remnant left to me of life, to the deserted worship of the Gods – the Gods of his fathers, the ever-bounteous – that blessed the world from the beginning of time, nor permitted our happy tribes to be afflicted with civil discord, till that fatal hour when the cursed Atlanthus was cast from the sea upon our shore. Within these far-spreading bowers, we were happy in our innocence; with the morning light, our songs, as cheerful as those of the birds, rose to the Powers that blessed us; at night, when our frugal meal was over, we stretched ourselves beneath the boughs, and dreaded no danger from the dishonesty of man, for we had nothing then that could be stolen. Spirit of Nature! did I say nothing? Yes - we had happiness and purity, and confidence in one another; but the sea-outcast has cheated us of them all."

"He has given us better," replied Arak: "he has taught us to improve our condition; the woes that wait on crime; the hope of a second life; and that a glorious morning will brighten in the rear of death. But the king summons you to come to him."

"What does he want?" said Icab, with a sigh. "I cannot aid him in his schemes. When I behold, through the opening woods, his rising towns, sad omens and presages darken my spirit, lest the Gods, whose secret throne of fires glows in the hollows of the mountains, burst forth, and sweep away the apostates and their perishable homes. But why does Oroon require me?"

"Arutha," replied Arak, "the queen, foregoes his love; and he desires that you would come with your skill, and restore to him her wonted affection."

Icab remained for some time thoughtful, and then said,

"Though she, too, is an apostate, yet I will go. Lead on: but never, save to take some gentle essence of herbs to quiet sorrow or to quench pain, shall my feet bear me to your city."

They then proceeded towards Atlantis, which when they entered, Icab looked around on every object with awe and superstitious dread.

Arak conducted Icab to Oroon, by whom he was received with filial affection, and who said to him that his appearance was as the cheering sun in the morning.

"Ah!" replied Icab; "and it has been night since we parted, and thou hast dreamt dreams in the woeful time."

"The sleep," replied Oroon, with a smile, "was yours. Like the bird that drowses in winter, and, awakening in the spring, finds nature renewed and full of blossoms and songs and life and joy, you came among us, wondering at the change. Would you have us resign the social arts and the pleasures industry makes ours, and have us sink back again into barbarity?"

"I wish," replied Icab, "only that you would cast off the vices which you put on with these gaudy garments: the virtues need no robes; they ever move in health and vigour, naked like our fathers. – But, Oroon, as I came to this stately dwelling, I beheld two great edifices – one too vast, too lofty, for any use of man; the other too grim and strong even for the most savage creatures of the wilderness. What are they?"

Oroon paused before he replied. "The first you spoke of is a temple hallowed to religious rites."

"What!" cried Icab, with pious horror. "Is, then, the God whom Atlanthus has revealed a local and limited being?"

"The God revealed to us," replied Oroon, "is the Father of nature, the Maker and Master of the ocean the heavens and the earth, and all things in them."

"Then, wherefore," said Icab, "have you built Him a house, when the universe is full of Him? In light, in blossoms, and in melodious sounds, we recognise his beauty: in fruits, in sleep, and in the gladness of the pure breast, we taste his bounty: the vast and inaccessible skies, with their infinitude of stars, bear witness to his greatness: in the strength of mountains, in the deep foundations of the mighty earth, and in the long fetching of his breath in the tempest, we acknowledge his power: and when we question why it is that we are, and all this world is, we discern his undiscovered nature. Is it to Him that ye have built a house?"

"Thou wilt but see our works," replied Oroon, "in thine own contrariety. We have not reared the temple for his dwelling, but as a place wherein we may holily remember that he exists and should be adored."

"Does your knowledge," exclaimed Icab, "your civilization, your science, your orders, and your ranks, tend to make you forget Him? Our fathers never dreaded such an accident. They heard him in the roaring of the seas, and in the wrath of the thunder: they dreaded the flapping of his wings in the storm: they hailed his smile in the dawn: they felt his kindness in the day; and, like tired children on their mother's lap, they trusted to him in their weariness, and fell asleep: He was every where with them, and they with Him. – But for what purpose is yon other edifice?"

"It is a prison," replied Oroon, blushing; "an appointed lodge for such as wrongfully injure each other."

"Stop, Oroon, stop," cried Icab; "retrace your steps back to your old simplicity. Already, your new found arts require inventions to remind you that God is; they have taught you to prepare for men that shall become, by these arts, more savage than the beasts of the woods: all this in a few short moons you have found already needful. Think what must be the end and issues of this civilization! If men already must be shut in dungeons, shall not the time come when there may be a race that must be put to death?"

Oroon made no reply, but only said, "Come with me and see Arutha, and, if you can, recal her love, which has long been ebbing from me."

He then conducted the old man into the apartment where she was sitting alone. Icab looked at her steadfastly for some time; he marked, with a keen eye, the manner in which she regarded her lord, and then said, with a stern countenance, "I do not think you, Arutha, ill of any corporeal disease, but some infection has tainted your mind. What wrong have you done to the kind Oroon, that you regard him with such aversion?"

"Be merciful," said Oroon; "think how dearly I once was esteemed by her. Yes: the recollection of our former affection, compared with the unhappy vacancy of this present estrangement, is like a playful child gambolling on the other side of a grave. Be kindly to her, and apply your remedies with the soft hand of your wonted gentleness."

"Oroon," said Icab, "I pray thee retire; I would converse with her alone."

When the king had left them, he said to Arutha sternly, "You fear Oroon - what wrong have you done to him, that you so shrink in his presence? Arutha, mark my words – the cause of your malady springs from something in this new condition of things. Why do you look in such amazement? Then it is true, and the apostacy has changed your heart. Oh! pause, and, before a blacker horror falls on you, abjure the subtle stranger's altars; and on the mountain's top, that higher, purer, unbuilt altar, by all-seen Nature raised to the all-felt God, lift up your hands, and deprecate your inconceivable doom!"

With these words Icab retired, and, meeting Arak, he bade him summon the elders of the tribes together. Atlanthus also came towards him, but he interdicted his approach, and accused him as the cause of miseries which were then impending over the country. At the same time Oroon came towards the, and, at his coming, Atlanthus obeyed the command of Icab, and retired. Oroon, who heard the command, said, "Now that he has gone, what have you to tell me?"

Icab looked at him with sorrow, and said, "The thunder in the summer's calm, and the Great Spirit in the woods and on the ocean, never speaks such horror as that which I must now declare."

"Tell me at once. Is my Arutha dead?"

"Curses descend on her!" cried Icab, extending his arms aloft. "Let fury come, and, as the winds scatter the leaves of the forest, disperse her guilty ashes!"

"Thou art mad, Icab," said Oroon, "and thou speakest ecstasies of looser thought than the wrack of clouds in the storm."

"The queen is false."

"False! What hast thou said? repeat the word – mine ears ring fearfully."

"Yes," said Icab, solemnly; "false with Atlanthus."

"Hoary liar!" exclaimed Oroon, as he struck him to the ground.

"Gods of his fathers," said the old man, as he lay at his feet, "accept my thanks for this. Now must his noble soul feel, by this dishonour in striking me, his own, his father's friend, what shame and woe, and evil and degradation, spring from the infection of the sea-outcast's guile."

Oroon stood like a statue for some time; and Icab rose and retired to meet the assembled elders, before whom he laid the proof of the guilt of Arutha and Atlanthus. She was sentenced to be placed on a rock, two bow shots from the shore, the head of which was only visible at half-tide: a boat, with a dumb man bearing a torch, was to convey her to the rock, and kindle a fire, the extinction of which by the tide, would show when the waters overwhelmed her. The sentence of Atlanthus was allotted to be pronounced by Oroon, whom he had so deeply injured.

Oroon would fain have avoided this dreadful task, but could not.

"Then," said he to the elders, "let Heaven punish him with health, and prolong his days, for he is noble, and the sense of guilt will be his punishment. Let no accustomed token of respect be withheld from him, lest the vindictive thought that springs from punishment defeat the intended horror of the sentence." Turning to Atlanthus, he addressed him with accents of the tenderest pity.

Arutha was then conveyed to the place appointed for her on the rock, and Atlanthus was taken down to the shore, where a vast multitude were assembled.

"What dost thou see?" said Oroon.

"A dim red flame."

"Nothing more? No sign?"

"Yes: ever and anon," replied Atlanthus, "it is eclipsed, as if some busy figure intervened."

"Arutha is there alone," said Oroon, in a deep and dreadful tone; and added, "does the light still burn?"

"It does."

"See you no other sign?"

"The swell of the rising tide rolls often between."

"Does it still burn? What means that universal sigh?"

"The light is quenched." In saying this, Atlanthus stabbed himself, and fell dead at the feet of Oroon.

"Stop!" exclaimed Icab; "touch him not, lest some new infection taint us from this hitherto unheard-of crime – self-murder. Now, Oroon, command the sacrifice – the atonement to thy father's gods."

At these words, Oroon called to the multitude to fire the town, and to burn all their works. This was done; and the Indians, throwing the garbs and vestments which Atlanthus had taught them to assume into the flames, abjured civilization for ever.

## THE END

# THE CAPTIVE

by

**Miss Susanna Strickland**
**(1814)**

## I

The starry diadem of night is gleaming
High over Cracow's ancient towers and walls;
And, like a spirit's silvery garment streaming,
From April's billowy cloud the radiance falls
Of the young moon, – through painted oriel beaming
On pictured galleries and pillared halls,
On helm and shield, and all the proud array
That fires the warrior for the battle fray.

## II

But there is one within that high saloon,
O'er whose crushed spirit Sorrow folds her wings;
Her downcast eyes heed not yon cloudless moon,
Her voiceless lip no joyous anthem sings;
Yet might her loveliness to rapture tune
The dullest spirit in the halls of kings:
Young, beautiful, and rich in artless grace –
What eye unmoved could gaze upon that face!

## III

On a low couch of India's splendid dyes,
In pensive attitude reclines the maid,
In motionless repose; one white hand lies

# THE CAPTIVE

On the small lute o'er which it lately strayed;
The other shrouds her face and streaming eyes,
And half uplifts the long fair locks that shade
The snowy beauty of that heaving breast,
Where Grief's wild billows swell and find no rest.

## IV

Again that graceful head is bent full low,
And all those glittering tresses downward sweep;
The starting tears in quick succession flow –
Oh! 'tis a luxury unrestrained to weep;
She feels a joy in that wild waste of woe,
Till o'er her wounded spirit balmy sleep
Gently descends, and veils that azure eye
Ere the bright tear-drop on its lash is dry.

## V

She sleeps; – and soon in fancy wanders far
Back to the much-loved land which gave her birth,
Forgetful of the cruel chance of war
That tore her rudely from her kindred's hearth:
Again, rejoicing 'neath eve's dewy star,
She leads the dance, and joins the voice of mirth,
And hears once more her native valleys ring
To sounds that make her light foot lighter spring.

## VI

And eyes are gazing on her – that have slept
Their last long sleep upon the battle plain –
Eyes that to welcome her with joy had wept –
Friends that had shared her rapture and her pain,
Brave hearts, that to defend her proudly leapt –
But found a grave among their people slain,
And left that lovely one in captive bands,
To pine away her life in foreign lands.

# THE CAPTIVE

## VII

She meets her mother's mild and melting glance
She hears her father, with a warrior's pride,
Bid the young beauty mingle in the dance;
Her sterner brother half in earnest chide,
As, bashful lingering, she would fain advance, –
Yet stops, – her conscious blushing cheek to hide;
While her delighted lover, pressing near,
Pours his impassioned suit upon her ear.

## VIII

She starts – she trembles! – and that heavy sigh
Already tells the gentle vision fled:
And, hark! – a martial step is echoing nigh –
A kindly figure bows him o'er her head.
Her slumbers vanish. With a fearful cry,
Her thoughts return to dwell upon the dead;
And she awakes to hopeless grief – to share
The victor's smiles – and hide her heart's despair!

# AFTERWORD

## Nick Ford

Since the dawn of oral history as a poetic tradition (if not earlier), groups of human beings settling on new land have, on clearing it to their satisfaction, encountered the remains and artefacts of people like themselves, the buried and forgotten settlements of unknown, unnamed strangers – and since place denotes community, these departed strangers from the past must somehow be explained, identified, and incorporated by some sort of adoptive process, into the new, incoming people's tribal annals, as a self-justificatory discourse.

Similarly, any still living occupants of the new land must be identified and explained by the incomers, in a way that integrates with the new tribe's myths, values and ideas of itself. The fictive musing over ancient remains and inscrutable autochthons is necessarily, the occupation of the Romantic poet no less than of the archaeologist or the anthropologist.

In these two works of early English-born Canadian literature we have, respectively, the curtain-call of two centuries' Romantic English dramatic attempts at such cultural accommodation which opened with Shakespeare's *The Tempest*, coming with Galt's *Apostate*, while Susannah Strickland's *The Captive* is among the last of the Romantic poems to employ the ancient paradigm of conquest in which the defeated nation is portrayed as a captive female, an idiom old as Euripides' *The Trojan Women*. Both, of course, are attempts to resolve the paradox of exploitative colonialism and native acculturation, with the supposed 'manifest destiny' of what is called Christian Civilisation – as well as, perhaps, the perceived, essential depravity of human nature. With Galt, savagery triumphs over Reason with regret for some earthly paradise of civilization irretrievably lost, as if Prester John had for a while won the Garden Of Eden back from the bush; while Strickland, had she set her poem in London rather than Cracow, could have been writing of the West Indian slave Mary Prince, whose biography she transcribed as an anti-slavery tract. In the poem, Strickland echoes the sighs of her captive with an authentic, personal sense of homesickness which is not merely literal, but spiritual – an alienation she was later to experience herself, when on her marriage to Lieutenant Moodie they left England to settle in Upper Canada.

Perhaps the strangest legacy of Galt's *Apostate* can be seen in the publication by Joseph Smith in 1830 of *The Book Of Mormon*, a year before Strickland's *History Of Mary Prince, A West Indian Slave* went into print: whatever we may think of their comparative merits, whether as literature or as original ethical-spiritual discourse, or whether Smith owes more of his work to Galt than to the angel Moroni, it is my belief that both Galt and Smith took up their pens in response to this need to invest the past with contemporarily-acceptable meaning or as Galt had it, if only in an imagined past and in the New World, "to find the arts of Europe / In sweet communion with the Christian faith" (*Apostate*: Act 1 Scene 2).

NICK FORD
Author
Southampton, United Kingdom

# ABOUT THE EDITOR

David J. Knight was born in Guelph, Ontario, Canada. He is an alumnus of Guelph and Southampton (UK). He is an internationally published author, with books and articles on Historical Biography, Archaeology and Archaeoacoustics, and was celebrated by the University of Guelph as a Campus Author in 2008, 2014 and 2015. Since returning to Guelph, he has written articles for *My Guelph* (2013) and published books with Publication Studio Guelph – *Sound Guelph* and an edition of John Galt's *The Omen* (2013). As the General Editor of Vocamus Editions he has also published *Guelph Versifiers of the 19th Century* (2014), a new edition of John Galt's *The Star of Destiny* (2015), and a new edition of Mary Leslie's *The Cromaboo Mail Carrier* (2016).